Connor's Little One

A Romantic Novel About a Daddy Dom who Trains His Baby Girl in the DDLG and ABDL Kink

By Tina Moore

Table of Contents

Chapter 1

The drive to the office was always mundane. What else could be expected with morning traffic? I could have avoided it altogether if I left earlier, but I didn't do that for two reasons. The first was that there was no way in hell I wanted to go to the office at all, much less earlier than was necessary. The second—related to the first in that I'd have to wake up earlier than usual—was that the term *morning person* didn't suit me in the slightest. Still, I suppose there were worse things as I pulled into the parking lot. I parked above ground because no one else did. It made the rush to leave a lot faster, albeit hotter when everyone who'd parked underground had to wait in a long line of cars as if they were getting some kind of head start on rush hour. Nevertheless, just because things could be worse didn't mean I had to enjoy them as they were. And I so didn't.

I probably wouldn't have hated the drive to work if I didn't hate my job so much, but the truth is that I hated my job. My position in life was boring, repetitive, and going nowhere slowly. The woman who raised me would have said I was a stubborn little brat, ungrateful for that which others would love to have, and perhaps she would be right. Perhaps I was ungrateful. Perhaps I should have been happier with my job. Perhaps things weren't so bad.

Only, as I walked into the office, I didn't care whether she was right or not. It was pretty bad as far as I was concerned. A musty smell, reminiscent of Grandma's old cupboards filled with mothballs, hit my nose and I knew I'd have to suffer through it all day. I spritzed a bit of my sweet-smelling perfume in the hopes that my own scent might distract me, knowing that I'd have to do it a dozen more times over the course of the day. The place buzzed and hummed with the sound of technology, computers and copiers and outdated fax machines all hard at work. Possibly the worst thing about the office was the color of the walls; a horrible sickly green that reminded me all-too-much of a doctor's office.

I didn't work in a doctor's office. I was not greeted with a waiting room full of sick, coughing patients. Still, a part of me wondered if it would have been a better environment.

No, my boss was not a doctor curing a world full of disease. Sure, he helped people, but the question was to what end?

At that moment, my boss materialized, walking through to his office—the one with a view and a door—in freshly polished shoes and a crisp navy suit. He didn't look at me as he passed by, but then he never did. Lawyers didn't look at their secretaries in this office unless absolutely necessary. Yes, secretary was my working title, complete with a small cubicle and a computer slower than the morning traffic. The man I worked for was a ruthless district attorney who defended, well, bad men.

"Slumming, I see," a voice suddenly spoke

over the top of the cubicle.

"Excuse me?" I looked up to find an incredibly pretty blonde woman staring at me, the corner of her perfect crimson lips curled into a smirk.

I didn't have to see the other side of the cubicle to know that Lisa was probably wearing a short dress that hugged her figure and matched her lipstick, worlds apart from me in my pantsuit. I knew the way to the top. The only problem was that I didn't want to reach it that way, especially not if my competition was Lisa.

"Oh, nothing," she waved her hand dismissively.

"You look tired today. Were you out last night?" She looked at me with her evil-looking eyes already knowing the answer.

"No," I answered blandly. Lisa knew I wasn't out last night. Lisa asked questions such as this one to goad me. Lisa would deny it, but she loved getting underneath my skin.

"I thought I saw you at the party, but I

guess not. Now that I think of it, that woman was wearing a really cute dress." Her pretty blue eyes roved up and down my body, taking in my pantsuit and old black pumps in a way that made my stomach turn.

"So, it couldn't have been you," she quickly added before flicking her hair. Before I could respond, Lisa turned and walked away, her hair swinging as she went. The light glinted off it, and I secretly reveled in the fact that it wasn't her natural color. Unfortunately for me, Lisa was too vain ever to let her roots start to show.

Needless to say, the start of my day was not a good one. For the rest of the day, I went through my duties while staring at the clock, wishing that time might go by a tiny bit faster. I had to resist the urge to slam things—my keys on the keyboard, my phone on its receiver, my fist through the computer screen. The only saving grace was that I was alone. My boss, Mr. Jones, didn't bother me. As much as I hated it, I did my job well, well enough that no one felt the need to check on me throughout the day. I might have been more inclined to leave my job as a secretary sooner if that were the case.

As it was, the day passed by slowly, and it was filled with the thought that I was bored and wasted in a law firm. By the time the clock finally ticked over to six p.m., I needed a drink. I was keenly aware of the fact that I was one of the first people out of the office and, due to my clever parking job in the baking hot sun, one of the first out of the parking lot too.

***

"Well, well, well," Connor murmured at the sight of me. He was drying a glass behind the bar, a glass I knew was just for me.

"It's been a while since I saw the likes of you here," he said, throwing the bar towel over his shoulder.

"The likes of me?" I raised my eyebrows, taking my seat in a barstool across from him, but it was hard not to smile.

"You've been a stranger lately, little miss,"

Connor said as he sat my drink down in front of me. It was my usual, a milkshake cocktail with more strawberries than alcohol, made just the way I liked it. The dimple in Connor's cheek appeared as I took a sip, reminding me for the thousandth time that my *baby girl* drink, as he called it, amused him to no end.

"Shut up," I mumbled shyly, color rushing to my cheeks.

"A woman can want both alcohol and a milkshake at the end of the day, you know," I said trying to assert my grown up authority. This only made Connor grin more.

"Oh, I never said that a woman couldn't," he mused, pursing his lips together to stop his smirk. Something about the way he said *woman* made me squirm in my seat as if I didn't quite qualify. Then again, I supposed it was difficult for anyone to look like an adult standing next to Connor, much less sitting across from him. The man was a giant, from his towering height all the way down to his tree-trunk thighs. He was built like a brick wall, and I was pretty sure he didn't even know how intimidating his appearance could be. Of course, then he would smile, and those dimples would come out, making butterflies swirl in the stomach of every woman within a five-mile radius.

"So? Aren't you going to tell me about all your woes?" Connor raised his eyebrows.

"What makes you think I have woes?" I questioned amused at his choice of words.

"Why else would you be here on a Monday night?" He replied, clearly impressed with himself.

Dammit. How much more obvious could I get? I looked around. The bar was quieter than usual, but that was to be expected for a Monday. I heaved a sigh and looked back to find that Connor was staring at me. If his expression could speak, it would be saying, "Uh-huh. That's what I thought."

"Okay, okay," I rolled my eyes before adding, "I have the Monday Blues."

"Don't roll your eyes at me," he murmured warningly.

"Now, get talking, little one," Connor said

leaning against the bar. I was used to this sort of behavior. Connor had been bossy from the day I met him. It was just the way he was. That didn't make me feel any less like I'd been reprimanded though, and so, I sipped my milkshake cocktail until there was nothing left.

"I'm listening," Connor stated. In his hand, he held another milkshake cocktail, which held my attention far more than he did.

"Don't even think about it. No talking, no milkshake," he teased, matching my exasperated expression.

"Fine. I had a shitty day at work. But there's nothing new there. I always hate work," I snapped.

And you for damn sure already know that, I thought to myself. I didn't miss the way he flinched when I swore. This time, however, he knew better than to call me out for my language. I wasn't sure what it was, but Connor hated it when I cursed or cussed. Truth be told, I went to the bar more often than I cared to admit, but could anyone blame me? There were alcoholic milkshakes, for goodness' sake! The music wasn't bad either, but nothing topped Connor and his sage advice. Don't even get me started on his heavy pouring hand. In truth, the bartender had become one of my best friends over the past few months. He was always willing to listen to me.

"Wanna talk about it?" He asked, softening, which only made me roll my eyes.

"There's nothing to talk about, really. I guess I'm just tired of going through the same old thing every day, you know? Life is so boring. I wish there were some kind of escape from it all," I replied, placing my head in my hands.

"And what if there was?" Connor almost interrogated. I looked at him and squinted my eyes.

"Was what?" I questioned, unsure of what his mysterious tone was hiding.

"An escape, little one. What if I told you that you could easily get away from it all and the only thing you needed was your imagination?" He asked simply. He slid my glass to me, and I started sipping, creating a pink, frothy, milkshake mustache on my upper lip.

"Sign me up," I laughed, happy to be getting my milkshake, dancing contently in my seat. Connor chuckled and grabbed a napkin, reaching across the bar to wipe the ice cream off of my lip. My breath caught in my throat at the close proximity. It wasn't fair that he was that much bigger than me. He barely had to lean forward over the bar to reach. It was difficult to concentrate on anything when he was that close and, truth be told, I sucked at holding my liquor. My head was as fuzzy as my tummy, and all I could think was that Connor was really warm. If I were anyone else, if I lived in any other life, I would have asked Connor out. But of course, I wouldn't. I was me, plain old Jessie, and there was no way a man like Connor would ever go for me. It's for that reason that I blame alcohol for what I said next.

"Are you just looking for an excuse to get close to me?" I teased, surprised at myself. Connor arched a brow, and I found myself staring into his striking blue eyes, holding my breath as I waited for the response.

"Do I need an excuse?" He asked, leaning back and showing off his big biceps.

Oh, my God. What am I doing? This is Connor! My mind was yelling at me as my eyes glazed over. The more I thought about it though, the more I thought this is Connor. He was tall, extremely good looking and always had the attention of some girl at the bar. Perhaps it was the fact that I knew him that made him so damn appealing, the way he was always there for me, and indeed even the way he was cleaning my froth mustache off at that very moment, though it made me feel small.

"You know," he finally continued, as if I weren't embarrassingly silent regarding his question. He continued to wipe my lip gently.

"I think I know just what you need," he said as he looked at me with an intense stare.

"Oh, yeah?" I asked with all the cheek I could muster while having a grown man wipe away milkshake froth from my face.

"And what's that?" I quickly added, trying not to slur my words.

"Well, for one thing, someone to put you in your place when you get cheeky," Connor said to my sheer surprise. I raised my eyebrows as he finally pulled back.

"Is that so?" I teased, not wanting to give up all my control over this conversation. Connor merely nodded matter-of-factly.

"You need a Daddy, Jessie," he said, making my head freeze as I heard him say my name. I made the terrible mistake of taking another sip of my drink and at his words, began coughing as it went down the wrong pipe. I could barely breathe as I spluttered, and before I knew it, Connor had hopped over the bar. His warm hand was on my back, gently patting, and was he cooing to me? It was getting too uncomfortable. I willed myself to breathe normally again and, with red and watery eyes, finally stopped coughing in time to catch my breath. I looked up at Connor, who seemed even larger on this side of the bar.

"What on earth are you talking about?" I said, shaking my head trying to focus on his words.

"I'm talking about a Daddy or a Daddy Dom more specifically," he began to explain. He tilted his head, and I could tell he was amused by my confusion. Apparently, I was funny. Who knew?

"And what exactly is a *Daddy Dom*?" I asked with probably more attitude than I should, considering the way he'd talked about putting me in my place. The thought alone made me shrink. I couldn't help but look Connor up and down. This was the first time there wasn't a bar between us, and well, it was kind of hard not to look.

"See, even if you don't know it, you still crave it," he said in a low voice.

"You want a Daddy who will tell you what to do, discipline you when you give too much attitude, and take you like you've never been taken before," he explained, sending a shiver down my spine. I didn't respond. I didn't know how to. All I knew was, for some reason, something deep within my center heated at his words. No, it wasn't his words. It was the way he said them. Close to me, close enough that I could feel his hot breath against the skin of my neck, and in an almost animalistic growl.

"You see, Jessie, I think you're a little girl deep down inside," Connor plainly said as he began to serve another customer.

Chapter 2

The morning brought with it several things. The sunshine filtering through my bedroom window, and the sound of birdsong woke me. Normally, these would have been welcomed, though when I felt the familiar throbbing of my head, I wished the silence of the night hadn't left. I'd have gladly rejected the sunlight too, my retinas complaining about the pain. At least I hadn't been woken by my alarm clock. My head might have exploded if that were the case. Thankfully, I was off work for the day. I wasn't so sure I would have had quite that many milkshakes the previous evening if I weren't.

How many had I had? I thought to myself. As my feet touched the floor, and I made my way toward the bathroom, everything came back to me. The memories were a blur at first, but by the time I'd climbed out of the shower, everything became startlingly clear, and I didn't know how to feel about it all. By the time I'd left the bar, I'd had three milkshakes, a couple of shots, and entirely too much Connor the Hot Bartender. Make that Connor the Daddy Dom as I now knew him.

The only problem was that I didn't know what a Daddy Dom was exactly. I mean, he tried to explain it to me, but by then, I was on my third milkshake and rather enjoying how close he was standing to me. It didn't hurt that he smelled really nice. I shut my eyes and groaned as more memories came back.

"And let me guess, you think you could be my Daddy? Put a Little Girl like me in my place?" I asked as I watched him shoot his whiskey.

"Oh, I don't think it. I know it." He had added as he watched me leave. I couldn't believe I'd asked such a thing. I'd always been a little flirty when I had too much to drink, and goodness knew I had a bad attitude. The few ex-boyfriends I'd had over the years called me a brat more times than I cared to count. Throw in a seriously attractive guy who seemed happy enough to flirt back, and I had a recipe for disaster. How was I ever going to go back to the bar again?

Still, regardless of my tipsy humiliation, Connor's words stuck with me, and I wondered what he meant by them. He didn't elaborate further, mostly because I hadn't asked, but in spite of myself, I was unbelievably curious. That's why the second I was dressed, I found myself sitting behind my computer with an incognito tab open. Little did I know it would be the first of many open tabs.

"What are you doing, Jessie?" I asked myself, heaving a sigh as I hit enter on the search bar. A thousand links regarding *DDLG* and *ABDL* showed up, and I quickly realized that the world was full of people practicing this particular kink. I would have expected a minority to be interested, but the overwhelming amount of information proved there were a lot more people into it than I'd initially imagined. And so, with no small amount of confusion, I began my learning journey. It was easy enough to find all the sexual stuff about the kinks, but what I didn't expect was the fact that it was clearly stated on every site that the relationship could be completely devoid of sex. I discovered that, as Connor had already told me, DDLG stood for Daddy Dom and Little Girl whereas ABDL stood for Adult Baby and Diaper Lover. They seemed totally bizarre at first, but the more I read, the more I found that they were incredibly loving relationships.

I was able to find some forums in which Daddy Doms and Little Girls actually communicated! Reading through them, I was astonished by the care plainly evident in the messages and questions. They were kind of cute, the longer I lingered. The Daddy Doms were caring and kind, taking care of their Littles as if they were legitimate children, and the Littles were carefree and happy.

The more I read, the more I wished I was as happy as they were. I searched why Littles were so happy, and that's when I found out about *Little Space*, a wonderful mindset that Littles went into at will. In this mindset, they thought and acted a younger age than they actually were. As far as I could tell, this varied from person to person and depended on their "age." Littles actually chose to act a specific age, any age they wanted, even two years old if that's what brought them joy. And they did the things that a person of that age did. This could be anything from coloring to wearing diapers.

One thing was clear to me though; Littles generally used Little Space to escape from the stress and troubles of their day-to-day lives. Simply put, they were people who enjoyed pretending to be younger than they actually were as a way to relieve themselves from their responsibilities. They shrugged their adult-self off in exchange for some carefree time doing something that made them happy, even if that was drinking from a baby bottle.

Biting down on my lower lip, I decided that was quite enough reading up on the kinks. My cheeks were hot, and I was consumed by an unexpected burning desire. To my shock, I really wanted to try

Little Space out. A small part of me didn't want Connor to be right, though after reading up on Littles, I was starting to believe that I simply wanted to rebel against him. Supposedly, Littles were supposed to be bratty. I didn't really like the idea of being nothing more than a stereotype. It made me pouty. A larger part, however, didn't care and kind of liked the idea of standing up to Connor, as if I was a brat.

I shook that thought off immediately. This was Connor. Yes, he was super attractive and sweet Connor, but he was also really bossy and intimidating Connor. And I didn't quite know how to feel about the heat that I felt in the pit of my belly at the idea of what Connor might do if I decided to stand up to him, especially after everything I'd read.

When did I start thinking about Connor as if he were a tasty morsel? I thought, a sudden rush of excitement flooding m veins.

I wasn't sure. Perhaps I'd always had some kind of hidden attraction for him. This realization only got me thinking about how Connor saw me. Was he attracted to me? If his flirting and that dominant way he'd breathed into my ear were anything to go by, that was a resounding yes. Had he always felt this way? I didn't know. The idea of someone like Connor looking at me as if I were a tasty morsel didn't seem possible.

Pushing thoughts of Connor and Daddy Doms away, I went back to thoughts of Little Space. After all, what could it hurt? I wasn't sure Connor was right about me needing a Daddy, but I definitely needed some kind of escape from my reality and from my horrible job in particular. Truthfully, I wasn't turned off by the idea of coloring books and, to my surprise, baby bottles. In fact, there was a lot that I wasn't turned off by in terms of the DDLG and ABDL lifestyle.

Once the computer was off, I made my way to my closet in search of something Little to wear. If I was going to try it out, this seemed as good a place as any. Absently, I wondered how things had changed so quickly. Only the day before, I was a normal person who drank too much when life got tough and hated my job. Now, I was trying on a bright pink dress dotted with yellow flowers in the hopes it might make me feel free.

The dress was tighter than it had been once upon a time, but as I twirled in the mirror, I had to admit that I looked and felt really cute. I giggled at my reflection, giving another twirl, this time stretching my arms out on either side of me.

The dress was sweet and innocent, frilly around the hem and modest around the neckline. It had been for a baby shower I once attended—the guests were all meant to dress in the adult version of something a baby girl would wear since the mother, a colleague named Caroline, was expecting a girl. At least I'd bothered to follow the dress code. Some of the guests had done the bare minimum, wearing their hair a certain way or bedazzling their dresses, if they'd made any effort at all. Looking back on it, I was the only one who'd put in a great deal of effort, going so far as to tie my hair into pigtails complete with pink ribbons. I didn't care that I got strange stares from the other guests. Caroline loved my outfit.

Pink ribbons. I'm sure I still have those around here somewhere, I thought running to my bathroom cupboard.

***

It was a Friday night, and that meant the music from the bar was loud enough that I could feel the bass vibrating through my tiny car where I was parked outside. Coming back here took a lot of courage, so much so that I didn't think I had any left to get out of the car. Yet I knew I was going to have to see him again sooner or later, not that I thought he would make some kind of arrangement to see me or that I would run into him at the grocery store. Such things had never happened before. I didn't expect them to start now.

However, I would be lying if I said that I didn't *want* to see Connor again. The fact of the matter was that I really wanted to see him again, probably more than might be considered healthy. It had been exactly one month since I'd been to the bar and discovered the truth about DDLG and ABDL, exactly one month since he'd told me that I needed a Daddy.

Since that day, I discovered a lot about myself. One of the things I discovered was that he was right. I needed a Daddy. After weeks of testing myself and exploring my Little Space, an act that involved no small amount of shopping I might add, I was certain that I was a Little Girl. He'd been right all along, and that begged the question: what else was he right about?

"Dammit," I sighed, slamming the palm of my hand down on the top of the steering wheel. That turned out to be a terrible mistake as I cried out in pain.

"Dammit!" I repeated as my hand now throbbed. Finally, I climbed out of the car and made my way inside. It was busier than the last time I'd been there but not nearly as busy as the nightclubs in the surrounding areas. That was one of the things I liked about the place. Based on the pounding bass, one would expect it to be packed.

Instead, it was filled with loyal regulars, and the music wasn't the usual electro stuff that could cause seizures even without all the flashing strobe lights. Classics played from a renovated jukebox in the back, hooked up to a massive sound system.

I spotted him the moment I walked in. He was talking to a leggy brunette in a skintight dress, and I felt the slightest twinge of jealousy. However, that faded away the moment he looked up at me. His hair complimented his eyes in the most flattering way, and his dimples came out as he smiled at me. It wasn't the cheeky smirk I was used to. This was a full-blown smile, showing off his pearly whites and touching his piercing eyes.

God, that smile was enough to make any woman's knees go weak, let alone a Little Girl's, I thought with a gulp. I stood up straight and walked over to the bar, resisting the urge to grin when the brunette looked me up and down. It was quite apparent that she noticed Connor's shift in attention. Against my better judgment, a surge of triumph shot through me, giving me the boost of confidence that I didn't know I needed.

Chapter 3

Any other day, I would have sat in a different seat. I would have waited for Connor to come to me for the sole purpose of pumping me with alcohol. I would have left the seat directly across from him, the one right beside the leggy brunette, empty.
There was something about the way Connor looked at me that night, though. I was filled with a certainty that his smile was meant for me and me alone, each of my steps leading me right toward it. When I took my place across from him, the brunette seemed to think as much as well because she got up with an indignant sound and walked away, after shooting both Connor and I a dirty look.

"I don't think she was a very happy customer," I pointed out.

"I'm afraid I accept tips based on the drinks, not the services… I might offer after hours," he stated, arching a brow.

"And I can tell you right now which one she was more interested in," he added. I bit down on my lower lip, unsure of how to respond. I wasn't sure what to say at all. Things had gone differently in my mind. I thought I could saunter up to the bar, though I'd never sauntered before in my life, and Connor would simply become putty in my hands. That clearly wasn't going to happen, and my hands were sweaty with nervousness.

"Can I get you a cocktail?" He offered.

"Yes, please." I didn't bother correcting him. We both knew they were milkshakes. Connor grabbed a glass and began preparing the drink.

"You look really nice tonight," he commented. "I especially like the hair."

"Yeah?" I asked. Warmth flooded my cheeks. I'd worn my hair in pigtails in the hopes Connor would like it, complete with pink ribbons. He nodded, watching me curiously as he slid my glass toward me and leaned over the bar.

"You know, I wasn't sure I'd ever see you

again. I kind of thought I'd scared you away," Connor confessed. I sipped my milkshake. The taste alone reminded me of the last time I saw Connor and everything that transpired between us. This time, there was no denying that I was attracted to the man. It was amazing how much had changed in such a short time. Perhaps I'd always been attracted to him somewhere deep in my subconscious. The fact that he was a different person to me now seemed as if it should have changed things. This was the guy who'd told me about DDLG and ABDL. Never in my wildest dreams did I imagine I might be sitting in front of him, pondering what it might be like practicing the kinks with him.

"I'm glad you came back," Connor broke into my thoughts, his voice barely louder than a whisper. It was the breathiness in his words that caused goosebumps to rise on every inch of my skin.

"And I'm proud of you," he said, making my stomach tighten, and my bottom lip be bitten involuntarily.

"You're proud of me?" I said softly, feeling excited, and nauseous all in one go.

"You heard me right," he nodded before adding, "I'm proud of you for doing your homework."

"My, my homework?" Suddenly, I felt exposed, as if he could see right through me.

"You know exactly what I'm talking about, little one," the stern tone of his voice sent my belly into yet another somersault.

"You did your research. And I'm proud of you," he simply said once again. In spite of myself, I grinned up at him. I was so happy that I could have danced around like a little kid. I didn't do that, of course. I had to maintain some kind of air of dignity and decorum. My feet might have done a little jig where he couldn't see them though.

"So, what did you think of your findings?" He asked, tilting his head curiously. For some reason, the fact that we were in a bar didn't matter. There were people all around us, and anyone could have eavesdropped on the conversation, but I didn't care. Everything faded away, except for us. The sound of the music, the dim lights, and the scent of alcohol no longer existed. The only thing that really mattered was Connor and me speaking casually as we had a million times before, even if the subject matter wasn't what one would call casual.

And yet, I had no idea how to answer the question at hand.

"I... uhm... well..." I stammered. I took a deep breath to steady myself and tried again.

"The truth is I'm kind of interested in it," I confessed looking down into my glass. Connor reached across the bar, taking one of my pigtails between his fingertips and stroking it lightly.

"I kind of figured that part out for myself. What I really want to know is what brought you back here. To me," he boldly said clearly impressed with himself. When he stood back up, he crossed his arms over his chest, and I could hardly gather my thoughts. They were too busy obsessing over how muscular his body was. His biceps bulged beneath the form-fitting black shirt he wore and the shirt itself hinted at the lines of strength that lay beneath.

"I want to learn more," I blurted out, causing him to arch a brow, this time at me.

"I want to learn more about it. And well, I figured who better to teach me than you?" I said, taking the biggest gamble of my life. The dimples in Connor's cheeks made an appearance, but the corners of his mouth only twitched as if he wanted to smile.

"Dinner. Tomorrow night. Wear a diaper," he said almost in dot point form. I stared at him, trying to figure out how to respond to that, but I had no words.

"It wasn't a question. I'm taking you to dinner. If you want me to teach you, I'm happy to, but there will be a contract with rules." This time, he did smile, and I felt almost as if I were prey to a predator.

"Do you agree to this, little one?" Connor

asked.

"I…" Taking a deep breath, I said the words I knew he wanted to hear, though I never expected them to make me press my thighs together the way I did.

"Yes, Daddy," I said breathlessly.

****

The first thing I discovered about adult diapers is that none of them were particularly flattering. The baby diapers were cute. They came in different colors, and some of them had images of teddy bears and candy and more all over them. If there was any chance they would have fit me, I'd have gotten them in a heartbeat, but alas, I knew they wouldn't, and it was with a somewhat heavy heart that I took a small pack of three adult diapers to the checkout station.

My heart raced as I stood in the aisle and glanced around to make sure that there was no one around who could recognize me. The last thing I wanted to do was give my colleagues more ammo to make my life difficult. It was a relief to know that the store wasn't busy early during my morning break on Fridays. I reached the cashier quickly, prepared to tell her some story about how I took care of my grandfather on the weekends, but she didn't so much as look my way until it was to tell me what my total came to. The only sound between us was the beep and the sound of her fingers as she keyed that amount into the computer system.

"Of course," I forced out over the lump in my throat as I pulled my card out and handed it to her.

"Would you like a bag with that?" She asked.

"Yes, please," I keyed in my pin. The rustle of plastic announced my exit as the cashier packed my diapers into a bag, and I walked out, trying too hard not to look suspicious.

***

Later that evening, I spent a great deal of time fidgeting in the mirror, convinced that my diaper showed no matter what I wore. Thankfully, the all-caps promise of the adult diapers being *noise-free* and *discreet* seemed to be true enough. I couldn't hear the shifting fabric as I moved. It was the lines I was more concerned with, not to mention the fact that I didn't look like I had an actual butt when I wore jeans. Clothes were strewn all over my bedroom, resembling some kind of closet massacre, evidence of my struggle to find something to wear.

Voices in my head were telling me disapprovingly that I should have bought myself a new dress, but there was one voice insisting that I pull out the clean white box in the bottom of my closet. Gold lettering marked the name of the dress boutique I'd gotten it from, and I traced the curly edges before eventually giving in, tugging the box I hadn't touched since high school out of its hiding spot. Inside was the dress I wore to my senior prom, a dress I only ever wore once, convinced that the feeling of glamor and prettiness that came with it would never be the same on any other night. I told myself that the dress wasn't something I could casually pull off. Now, however, it seemed I had nothing more suitable to wear on my date—an actual date with Connor the Hot Bartender!

When I opened the box, frills and smooth silk was revealed. It was impossible to resist the urge to reach out and touch the soft fabric, brushing my fingertips along the pretty lilac material. Nerves danced through me at the idea of wearing the dress again, but as I pulled it out of the box, unfurling the delicate cloth, my heart soared excitedly. The next thing I knew, it was zipped up my spine, and I was doing small twirls in the mirror. The dress flared at the waist into a waterfall of frills, which meant it didn't cling to the areas where the diaper would be, ended just above the knees, and it was shoulder-less, revealing the barest hint of cleavage beneath my favorite heart pendant. To complete the look, I added an innocent pair of white lace thigh-highs—another item from my high school closet—and a pair of matching wedges. I styled my hair into soft curls and kept my makeup natural.

Before long, it was time to climb into my car to meet Connor. I typed the address into my GPS, and I was off. He'd texted me the name of the restaurant upon my reluctance to let him pick me up. It was the first date, after all, and I didn't exactly know Mr. Hot Bartender as anything but a bartender. Seeing him outside of the bar was going to be an interesting experience. The thought made my core tighten, and I was pretty sure I was blushing by the time I reached the restaurant. He was probably—and by that, I mean definitely—the most attractive guy I'd ever gone out with. Throw in the kinky stuff, and he was close to being the most attractive guy ever.

***

The restaurant was on the nicer side of town, and it was even fancier on the inside than it was on the outside. There was a stage in the back of the restaurant, and a live band played lowkey jazz music, creating a classic feel when combined with the tasteful décor and candles on every table. As soon as I walked in, I was relieved that I'd decided to wear the prom dress. Cocktail dresses and suits surrounded me. I knew I'd have felt extremely underdressed in anything else that I owned.

A hostess dressed in a figure-hugging crimson dress walked over to me, her hair and makeup was immaculately done to such an extent that I suddenly understood why men struggled to speak when near attractive women. I could barely find the words even after she offered a husky, "Hi, do you have a reservation?"

"I... uh... I think so?" I stammered. She raised her perfectly shaped eyebrows, "Name?"

"Uhm..." I said, looking around.

Oh shit. I don't know what Connor's last name is, I thought to myself, feeling stupid for not knowing.

"Do you have a name?" The hostess repeated, growing impatient.

"The reservation is under Anderson," a deep voice boomed from behind me. I spun around at the same time as the hostess looked up. We were both wearing heels, and Connor was still taller. He looked taller than he had on the other side of the bar. My eyes roved over his entire body, and it was obvious that Connor spent a lot of time in a gym. I wasn't complaining. On the contrary, I nearly had to wipe the corner of my mouth as it watered. Never had I imagined Connor in a suit, but he looked incredibly sexy, and it clung to him in all the right ways.

When Connor gave me a smile, my heart beat a tiny bit faster. His eyes traveling over my body made it worse. I could tell he liked my dress.

"Hey," I murmured in a small voice.

"You're absolutely breathtaking," he wrapped an arm around my waist.

"Ah, Anderson," the hostess said. "Of course. Right this way, please."

We followed her to a private booth near the stage. The lighting was dim, and the space was intimate. Connor and I sat across from one another, and the hostess handed us a menu each. At first, I felt excited and warm about being in such a nice place, but once we were actually seated, all sorts of thoughts and realizations came to mind. For one thing, the awareness that I had a diaper on had all but faded until this particular point of the evening. We were in such a public place, and we weren't here for a normal date. No, we were here to talk about a contract.

I'd done some research on contracts as part of this lifestyle, so I was sure I'd be fine, but what if someone noticed how unusual our meeting was? The idea of being around so many people made me far more nervous than I would have liked to be.

"Could we get a bottle of your finest chardonnay and one strawberry milkshake with a tumbler of vodka and a tumbler of gin?" Connor ordered before the hostess could leave.

"Of course," the hostess gave a tight smile.

"I'll have your waiter bring it over," She said plainly. When she walked away, I turned to Connor.

"I don't think she was happy that you ordered so soon," I whispered.

"Too bad," he shrugged, looking at me

intently.

"She's not my concern," Connor replied, taking my hand in his.

"Oh?" I offered. I knew he was talking about me, but I wanted to be sure. He reached into his jacket pocket and pulled out a thin folder.

"I came prepared. Did you?" He said, raising an eyebrow at me. I nodded my head, my tongue darting out to moisten suddenly dry lips, unable to bring myself to confirm with words. He didn't have to elaborate. I knew exactly what he meant, and it made me shift slightly, remembering what I was wearing beneath my dress. I began to flip through the pages of the menu in the hopes that it might distract me. Plus, I was always one of those people who hated ordering, worried I was going to fumble over my own tongue or something. It wasn't exactly what I would call an impossibility, as proven by years of past embarrassing moments.

"Good," he smirked approvingly, opening the folder.

"Now, you've reminded me of something,

little one. It has to do with a rule I've put in the contract. Would you like to know what it is?" He said, a wicked gleam in his eye. Did I want to know what it was? My body was buzzing with the anticipation! I nodded my head slowly, trying to keep from showing just how excited and a more than a bit nervous I really was.

"Come over here," Connor inclined his head toward the spot next to him, and I happily shimmied over to the other side of the booth. I was rewarded with, "Good girl." Our drinks arrived then, carried on a tray by a man younger than me, dressed in a crisp tuxedo.

"Your drinks," he said in a suave voice as he set them down. He held the tray up beside his head in a way I'd never seen waiters do outside of film.

"Are you ready to order?" He added after placing our drinks down.

"I am. I'll have the Bouillabaisse," Connor turned to me.

"How about you?" He said, looking at me. I looked between the two of them. My voice caught in my throat. Why did he have to go and put me on the spot like that?

"I... uh..." I stammered. Connor smiled at me and leaned in to whisper in my ear. I nearly lost the ability to speak altogether because his breath was hot, where it tickled the most sensitive part of my neck.

"You know, you could just point, and Daddy will order it for you if you can't pronounce the names, baby girl," he lovingly said. Parts of me I didn't expect to react to such a comment pulsed in response and heat spread out across my chest. Still, I found myself reaching for the menu and pointing out the item.

"She'll have the Coq au vin," Connor turned back to the waiter.

"Thank you," Connor said, dismissing the waiter.

"I'll get right on that," the waiter bowed his head slightly and walked away with absurdly good posture.

"Right," Connor turned back to me.

"Shall we get back to it?" He half-laughed.

"Yes, please," I replied, feeling more overwhelmed than I wish I did.

"Ah! She speaks!" Connor grinned as I shrank into my seat, blushing.

"So, I've made a list I wanna go over with you. We're going to go over some things that you do and don't want as a part of this agreement, and after that, you can tell me if you wanna take a look at the rules I wrote for you to follow," he explained.

"I have to follow rules?" I asked, my eyes widening. I'd read about Daddy Doms giving their Littles rules, but I didn't know how serious Connor was about all this stuff. A lot of the posts referred to fake Daddy Doms, and I had a feeling I was getting the real deal when it came to Connor.

"Mhmm," he hummed.

"So, I want you to tell me if there's anything I should know before we get into this. Are there any health conditions or triggers that you have?" He asked sipping his drink. I just shook my head.

"Okay, we know your experience is definitely on the beginner side," he said pointing out the obvious. How could I argue? He looked back down at the folder.

"We'll have a safe word too. I'm thinking either *cinnamon* or *pineapple,*" he suggested. "Cinnamon!" I cried out so loudly that several people stared at us. I ducked my head.

"Sorry, I really love cinnamon pancakes," I explained. I thought he would be surprised or even annoyed, but the dimples appeared in his cheeks, and I could tell he was amused.

"Cinnamon, it is," he murmured before continuing, making a quick note in the contract.

"Okay, in that case, I want you to just tick these off for me. We should keep a record because if at a later stage, there are things you want to try or don't want to do anymore, we can simply refer back. You know?" Connor explained as I was busy taking it all in.

"Okay," I took the pen he held out for me,

and he slid the folder over. There was an entire checklist of potential acts we could perform, including oral only, soft petting, light sexual activity, and full sexual activity. I looked over at Connor, and if I had any doubts before, his eyes set me at ease. I checked full sexual activity. As I went through the rest of the list, I felt Connor's hand on my inner thigh, slowly edging its way up and beneath my skirt. I bit down on my lower lip as I checked things off. With each tick, Connor's fingers moved further and further up until I could feel his hand against the diaper, and it should have been weird, but it wasn't, not even remotely. No secrets. Non-negotiable. I bit down on my lip. That was a tough one. Check. Diapers. Check. Public display. Well, this was one, wasn't it? Check. Spanking. Check. Collaring. Was that like, ownership? I had seen some cute collars in my research. Check. Connor's hand was so high that my skirt was wrapped around my waist, and his fingertips were already dancing across my waist, teetering around the waistband of the diaper. My heart was racing, and I could barely concentrate on the paper in front of me. Goosebumps rose in the wake of his touch.

"Go on," he whispered. I bit my lip and went back to the list. After all, it didn't seem like Connor was going to take things any further unless I finished. That made sense. It was a contract. What I didn't expect was that I really wanted to see where he was taking things.

Must eat three times a day. That was easy enough. Check. Enforced bedtimes, check. Double-check. Enforced outfits. Check. I wondered if Connor would buy me special Little outfits. I'd already started a wish list: restriction and bondage. I looked over at him, my hand hovering over the checkbox.

"You could always half-tick it, and we know that's a maybe," Connor said.

"I can do that?" I excitedly asked. He nodded his head. With a smile, I half-ticked the checkbox. Soon, I was all done with the main agreements and Connor took the pen so that we could sign it. There was a special signature line for the Little Girl and the Daddy Dom. It struck me at that moment how real what we were doing was. It gave me a thrill, and I found myself moving closer to Connor.

Our meeting was momentarily halted by the arrival of the food. The waiter brought it on a bigger tray, placing our food in front of us. Without another word, he disappeared, and I raised my eyebrows.

"They have weird service here," I said, looking at the fancy meals in front of us.

"These tables are for people who want privacy," Connor explained.

"They won't approach unless absolutely necessary, and when they do, they're discreet," he said before gesturing for me to start my meal.

"Oh. That's a thing?" I asked, curious about how he knew about this type of service. He nodded his head, but the way he was looking at me told me that waiters were the last thing on his mind.

"So, you're officially my Little Girl," Connor

said calmly, but I could tell he was impressed with himself. The words ran around my head and in spite of everything, I wanted more than that.

"What... does that mean exactly?" I said, surprised at the speed we were taking things.

"What do you mean?" Connor asked, looking up from his meal.

"Just... well, does being your Little Girl mean? Do we only do what the contract says, or is there more to it?" I asked. Connor leaned in, looking me in the eye.

"Do you want there to be more to it?" He slowly said. Did I? With him so close, I could see the tiny hazel flecks that dotted his eyes, and I found myself wondering how I'd never noticed them before. Years, I'd been going to that bar, and it wasn't as if I'd only ever gone for the drinks. Don't get me wrong, they were amazing, but I'd gone for Connor. I went to talk to him because he was one of the only things that made me smile at the end of a horrible day.

I took a deep breath.

"Yeah, actually. I do," I said more confidently than I knew I could be. To my surprise, Connor smiled.

"Yeah? Me too," he stated, a smirk of happiness forming in the left-hand side of his mouth. The words brought a smile to my face, and butterflies fluttered in my belly.

"Really?" I almost squealed. Connor took my hand in his free one and squeezed it gently.

"Would you like to be my girlfriend, Jessie Phillips?" Connor formally asked.

"Wait, you know my last name?" I gasped. The corners of his mouth twitched with amusement.

"Believe it or not, I do remember the first day you walked into the bar," he confessed.

"Oh," the tips of my ears went red with heat.

"Right. Yeah, no, I'm gonna go ahead and blame alcohol for my memory loss," I said trying to give myself an excuse. At this, Connor burst out laughing. It was warm and safe and rumbled through his belly.

"You're adorable, but then, you always have been," he said before kissing my cheek.

"I wanna be your girlfriend," I blurted out.

"I can't tell you how happy that makes me, little one," he whispered, squeezing my hand again.

"How about we go through the rules?" He suggested. He handed me a new list. This time, when I took the pen from him, Connor slipped his opposite hand beneath the waistband of the diaper and moved lower and lower until I could feel his fingertips grazing the most sensitive part of my body. I gasped as my clit pulsed in response.

"Keep reading, baby girl," Connor whispered. I only hummed in response, turning back to the list. Some of the rules were repeats of the things I'd checked in the contract, such as enforced outfits when Connor and I were together, and I went into Little Space. My bedtime would be ten p.m. I wasn't allowed to swear. That one made me giggle, but that was cut off as Connor began moving his finger in small, circular motions and it was hard not to moan.

"Yes, I agree to the rules. All of them," I gasped. Biting down on my lower lip, I glanced around to make sure that no one was looking at us and I was surprised to find that they weren't. We were, as Connor had said, in a completely private space. And he was taking full advantage of that because the next thing I knew, one finger was inside me. It wasn't like it had much of a struggle. I wasn't sure that a man had ever made me this excited.

"So wet," Connor murmured approvingly.

"Is my little girl enjoying herself? Does this turn her on?" Connor whispered in my ear.

"Answer me, Jessie," he pressed, moving his finger in and out at an achingly slow pace.

"Does the idea of Daddy fingering your pussy out here in the open, in public, get you all worked up?" He nipped the top of my ear and as he continued to move his finger in and out of me.

"Your pussy certainly likes it. Doesn't it?"

He continued. The edge in his voice was enough for me to force out an answer, though it came out breathy and high-pitched.

"Yes," I moaned, rolling my head back as he worked his magic.

"Yes?" He questioned. I looked down at the list. Right at the bottom, I'd already read the very last rule. It was a condition that I had to answer and thank Connor in one specific way.

"Yes, *Daddy*," I whispered.

"There's a good girl," Connor added a second finger and began thrusting them in and out of me much faster than before. I could barely breathe as the pressure in the pit of my belly built and built, taking me higher and threatening to explode.

"Give yourself to me, little one. Show Daddy how much you want him. Do you know how much I want you?" He coaxed as he edged me closer. I shook my head; my curls whipping against my face and clenched my thighs together. My orgasm was within reach, and my hips were moving up to meet

Connor's hand, trying to get more of him.

"I want you so much that I'm as hard as a fucking rock right now," he whispered, pressing a kiss to the curve of my neck. With his free hand, he moved mine toward his crotch, and I could feel the obvious bulge through his pants.

"And I can't tell you how much I wish I could bend you over this table to show you what you do to me," he whispered, kissing my cheek.

"Oh, fuck," I gasped. And just like that, Connor's hand was gone. I tried to grab onto it, but Connor was far stronger. I may as well have been a fly for all my efforts.

"Wait! Why?" I complained.

"Because I have to punish you for breaking your first rule," Connor shrugged nonchalantly. His finger still glistened as he reached for a napkin to wipe his hand. As I watched, he closed the folder with the documents signed by both of us and put it back into his jacket before he picked up his knife and fork and began casually eating as if nothing were out of the ordinary.

"Eat your food, little one," he said as if not moments ago he was about to make me explode. Every part of me wanted to argue, but instead, I settled into my meal. It was an argument I knew I was going to lose. The rules were agreed to only moments before. I shifted uncomfortably for the rest of the meal, pressing my thighs together as if it might provide some form of relief. It was nothing compared to the expert way Connor's fingers danced along my center. I had to admit the food was good, though.

***

After the meal, Connor and I went back to his place. He drove my car because it was easier than having to tell me where he lived. Plus, he had no excuse not to touch me in the passenger seat and boy, did he touch me. My body was tingling from head to toe by the time we reached his house, mostly because all he'd offered were teasing brushes against my breasts and inner thighs, never going further, never touching me the way I really wanted to be touched.

When did I become such a slut? No guy had ever made me so hot for him before. I barely knew Connor—technically I'd known him for over two years, but this was different—and yet, he could have gotten me to beg for him if he wanted. That's how badly I wanted him.

The moment we got into the house; I was bent over the back of a couch. I barely had a second to take in the house around me. The sound of the door closing was accompanied by the feeling of Connor pressed up behind me. I could feel the bulge in his pants, pressed right against me, with the diaper between us.

"Do you know why I'm punishing you, Jessie?" He asked.

It was so rare for Connor to use my name that I knew I was in trouble.

"Yes, Daddy," I obediently said.

"And why is that?" He asked.

"Because I said the F-word, Daddy," I replied, knowing my mistake. Connor's hands pulled the diaper down, and I felt the cool breeze hit my bare ass. His hands stroked the firm flesh and right when I thought I was okay; he raised one hand and brought it back down. The sound of his hand slapping my butt echoed in the space, and I cried out in both surprise and pain as the heat rushed to the spot. I was sure he'd left a handprint. I didn't have time to linger on the first smack though.

"Count," Connor said. He didn't give me a chance to register what he'd just said before his hand came back down on the other side. I cried out.

"Count!" He growled.

"Two!" I squealed before adding, three, four, five, six, seven." By the time he was done, both my cheeks were red and stinging, but I knew Connor had taken it easy on me because I didn't need to cry, even though I felt awful for having broken a rule. Connor stopped smacking my ass and flipped me around, taking me into his arms. I was breathing heavily, and each movement burned a little.

"I won't break the rule again, Daddy," I said in a small voice.

"You won't?" He looked down at me, tucking a loose strand behind my ear. My face was warm, and even after I'd been spanked, I closed my eyes and leaned into Connor's gentle touch against my cheek. Connor pulled me into him and held me for a while. I found myself thinking that punishments weren't so bad if this was what followed them. We stayed like that for quite a while, until my ass stopped stinging and I didn't feel so guilty anymore. I was coming back to myself. The next thing I knew, his lips were on mine, and we were kissing. He coaxed my mouth open and drew a moan out of me when his tongue touched my lower lip.

"You took your punishment so well, little one," he finally said when he broke away.

"I'm really proud of you, and I wanted to wait to show you this, but I think you deserve a reward. I have some presents for you," Connor said, his face matching his words.

"Presents?" I clapped my hands together happily. Connor beamed and walked over to the dining room table. I took in the clean, light, and airy décor. His place was actually really nice and surprisingly neat. I'd have thought a big brawny man like Connor would have lived in a man cave, but it seemed that was not the case. He came back with a gift bag full of gifts for me.

Taking it from him, it was impossible to keep the excitement down. My Little was out in full force, and she had presents! I opened the gift bag and inside was a variety of things, including a fluffy bunny onesie, a coloring book, and a pink pacifier. These were all on my wish list of Little things, and I couldn't believe this was really happening. I didn't think I'd ever been so happy.

"Oh, my gosh, I love them!" I gasped.

"What does my little girl say?" Connor said as he pulled me onto his lap.

"Thank you, Daddy!" I clapped my hands together.

Chapter 4

For the first time in months, I didn't mind being at work. Throughout the day, all I could think about was Connor, and that kept me in a state of hopeful bliss. It was a Friday evening, the first that Connor had off since we'd gotten together. Bartenders apparently never got weekends off, but he had some kind of a surprise for me. Seeing Connor was exciting enough, but I couldn't wait to find out what it was he had planned.

The last time Connor surprised me; he took me on a shopping spree. As a result, I had several new Little outfits that we kept at his house and a few toys. Thus far, we hadn't gotten anything more than that, but getting to wander around dressed like a Little was some of the most fun I'd ever had. The fact that I had someone who could simply let me be while I colored in one of my coloring books was incredible, and I never understood how freeing it would be. Every time I'd wished I were still a child, wished that life was still as simple as it had been back then.

Connor helped show me that it really could be.

"What are you so giddy about?" Lisa asked me the moment I walked into the office, wincing at the sight of me. I simply beamed, ignoring her and headed to my desk. Even Lisa, Queen of all that was bad, couldn't get to me that morning. The day passed by quickly enough with intermittent texts from Connor. He didn't like that we often text while I worked. He said it hindered his good little girl's productivity. When the day ended, Lisa tried to take one last jab at me.

"Are you excited to go home to your life of loneliness? You do know there's more out there than just your bed, right?" She sneered. Gosh, I hated this woman.

"I'll actually be in my boyfriend's bed," I happily sang as I walked out, leaving the office. I didn't look back at her, but I wished I could have seen the look on her face. Little Space and Connor had both instilled a newfound confidence in me, and I felt as if nothing could touch me—not even Lisa. I was still beaming when I got to the car, and by the time I arrived at Connor's house, my cheeks were aching from smiling. Who would have thought?

***

Connor opened the door before I knocked. He was wearing a pair of worn blue jeans that hung off his hips in just the right way and a white T-shirt that was too tight around the biceps, but loose enough that one couldn't quite see all the rippling muscles beneath it. Before I could overthink it, I reached for him, my hands slipping beneath the hem and moving up his sides.

"Uh-huh. Hello to you too," Connor said with a grin.

"Hey, Daddy," I sang, taking my hands out only to run them down over the waistband of his jeans.

"What are we doing tonight?" I added, hoping that I would get want I wanted.

"Now, as much as I wish that was in the plans," he took both my hands in his, intertwining our fingers.

"I'm taking you out. And I want you to wear one of the outfits Daddy bought for you," he said before kissing my cheek. He stood to the side, and I entered the house, letting go of his hands. "I have to wear one of my outfits out?"

"Mhmm," he nodded.

"Go on. We're gonna be late if you don't get ready soon," Connor said more sternly. I hesitated; my feet glued to the ground. Why did I feel as if I'd been thrown right into the deep end? Suddenly, I wasn't too fond of the idea of a surprise. If I knew where we were going, I could either return to my prior state of bliss or I could say I didn't want to go. Was that too much to ask for?

"Little one," Connor walked over to me. I was surprised to find that he wasn't using his stern voice.

"You're going to love it. Don't you trust Daddy?" He said making me blush. Did I trust

Daddy? I wasn't sure I trusted anyone. I mean, it isn't as if the world gave me much reason to trust anything in it. If I had to choose one person, though, it would definitely be Connor.

"Yes, Daddy," I replied, finally making up my mind.

"Good. Now run along," he said, playfully slapping my ass. I raced toward the second bedroom where we kept all my things. It was easier than trying to find space somewhere in Connor's room. I think he liked having a space that was still his. Tugging the chest of drawers open, I was astonished by the sheer amount of stuff that Connor had gotten me. It hadn't all been on our shopping spree. Rather, small things had been added over time, and now I had a great collection. How was I supposed to choose anything to wear?

It was our first date all over again. I pulled three onesies out, but I hadn't been out in my pajamas since I was a little girl. I wasn't so sure that I was ready for that one quite yet.

Little by little, I crossed off the outfits that I wasn't

willing to wear out in public. Eventually, I ended up with a denim overall and two dresses. Most of the time, dresses were what I wore when I was with Connor. I didn't really want to wear them out. That left the overalls and a cute white T-shirt.

When I walked out with my thumbs beneath the straps and my hair braided into pigtails, Connor looked up from where he sat on the couch and smiled at me. My heart instantly swelled under that gaze. I knew what he was about to say before he said it and it brought a ready smile to my lips.

"Good girl!" Connor exclaimed, his eyes telling me all I needed to know.

***

I was blindfolded the entire way there. I tried to count the turns to figure out where we were going. In the back of my mind, I hoped that we wouldn't be going anywhere familiar. If it was somewhere, I'd been before. I wasn't sure I was going to enjoy this surprise.

Eventually, I had no choice but to give up on figuring it out. Somewhere along the way, I'd miscounted a turn. We could have been in a different city for all I knew. Music played along the drive—an album Connor knew I loved—and I lost all sense of time. Before we arrived, the scent of cake seemed to linger in the air. I shrugged it off, thinking the blindfold must have been messing with my senses. I was just hungry, and my nose imagined what my belly craved.

If I thought Connor would remove my blindfold when we got there, I was wrong. Once we arrived, he parked and came around to lift me out of the car. Then, like some kind of newlywed couple, he carried me toward the place, and only afterward did he finally take my blindfold off.

"You ready?" He asked before untying it. I nodded my head excitedly, and I could see at long last. Lucky for me, the light was dim, and it didn't hurt my eyes as they adjusted to it. The first colors to hit my retina were pink and purple. Everywhere I looked, the pastel colors that Littles seemed to be so fond of hit me. There were too many other women—no, girls—to count, all of them dressed in

Little outfits. Lace, pastels, and innocence speckled the room. Even so though, there were a few who were darker shadows in the space, as cute and Little as the rest. I didn't even know there was such a thing as a Little who expressed their happiness through the color black but seeing the diversity all around me made my heart feel light. The corners of the room, painted in a sweet pattern of pinks and whites, were packed with hundreds of stuffies. Off to the distance, I could see several other Littles having tea parties or playing with dolls in forts. It looked better than any play place I'd ever visited as a kid, and I was ecstatic. I knew I was deep in Little Space, and this place was the biggest trigger. The words Connor said before all this started came to mind, the way he knew exactly what a 'Little Girl' such as myself needed. Out of the corner of my eye, I knew Connor was happy with my response, but I had more important concerns.

"Daddy, can I please go play?" I said, practically hopping up and down.

"Sure, little one. But remember that this isn't the only room," He explained. I'd been ready to run off, but I stopped at the sound of that.

"There are other rooms?" I asked, curious about what I would learn tonight.

"Of course. There are play sessions happening, spa sessions, and plenty of different aged rooms," Connor continued to explain.

"That's so cool," I breathed, my eyes wide as saucers.

"Do you wanna take a walk through them?" Connor asked, taking my hand in his. At that, I froze for the first time. The rooms were interesting enough, but I didn't want to walk through them right now. There was a table with a group of three girls coloring, and every part of me wanted to be there with them. I knew this was a judgment-free zone. I could always go look around later. I shook my head, my pigtails flying.

"I wanna go color," I said, biting my bottom lip. Connor's mouth twitched, but he didn't quite smile even though I could see the joy in his eyes.

"Okay, go have fun. I'm gonna go get us something to eat," he said turning on his heel. I looked over at the table of food. There was cake. Without wasting another moment, I moved toward the coloring table as quickly as I possibly could. The three other girls looked up as I approached, and at the sight of one of them, my heart sank to the pit of my stomach. The blood drained from my face, and it felt as if the temperature had been turned down to sub-zero. I knew one of those faces. Lisa.

Chapter 5

"Oh, what do we have here?" Lisa stood from the table, wearing a frilly white dress paired with pink thigh-highs and a pink collar. My mouth was suddenly dry.

"Little Jessie. This is too precious," she said, delight in her eyes. I could barely move as Lisa walked around me, taking in my outfit with a smug look on her face.

"Wh... what are you doing here?" I stammered.

"Come on, Little Jessie," Lisa rolled her eyes.

"I know you're not that stupid. I'm here for the same reason as you. I just, you know, do it better. But that's nothing new, is it?" She said smirking at me. My happiness was dashed in mere moments. Of all the people to be here, to find out about my secret, why did it have to be her? I hated Lisa with a passion, and she knew it because I was pretty sure she hated me just as much. And based on the way Lisa's eyes were glittering with malice, I'd have hazarded a guess that she definitely wasn't willing to change her ways because she found out we were both Littles. On the contrary, I had a feeling that things were about to get so much worse.

"Is this really the best you could do?" Lisa suddenly asked. She reached out to take the tip of one of my pigtails, grimacing.

"How tacky," she spat out at me. Looking around, I knew I wasn't the only girl with braided pigtails. Lisa was just trying to get to me. I wished it wasn't working. At the coloring table, the other two girls were watching us with wide eyes, their coloring pencils still in hand.

"I know!" Lisa clapped her hands together.

"How about you let me do your hair, Jessie? I bet I could make it look really pretty, better than the mess it is right now. And you should totally take off your clothes," she said, making me nervous.

"Excuse me?" I asked, backing away as she tried to untie one of the pink ribbons in my hair.

"Yeah, there are rooms where you're allowed to do that. Playrooms, you know?" She gave me an evil grin. As sweet as her voice sounded, my instincts were on red alert. It was too sickly sweet.

"I could show you," she said, getting aggressive.

"No thanks," I shook my head, turning away. As I did, Lisa grabbed hold of one of my braids and yanked me back. I cried out in pain, and both the other girls at the table jumped upward, trying to pull Lisa off of me. She was stronger than she looked, and she refused to let go. My eyes were stinging with pain, and I shut them tightly. The last thing I wanted to do was let Lisa see me cry.

"Hey! Let go of her!" Connor's voice rang out. Suddenly, my hair was released, and I felt the strong arms of my Daddy as he wrapped them around me, pulling me to him. I opened my eyes, expecting to see his eyes filled with worry, but that didn't happen. Instead, Connor was staring at Lisa as if he'd seen a ghost. When I glanced over at her, Lisa had a similar expression on her face.

"Wait," Lisa murmured in a small voice.

"You're Jessie's Daddy?" Lisa said, almost choking on the words. Oh, no, no, no, no. It was obvious. They knew each other. I wasn't the only one who knew Lisa. Even worse than that, they knew each other in these circles. My mind raced, and I was putting puzzle pieces together that I hoped didn't fit. But then Connor spoke in a stern voice that I recognized from the few times I'd been punished and reprimanded.

"What the hell is wrong with you, Lisa? I'm ordering you to leave Jessie alone. Don't come anywhere near her," Connor growled. The smallness disappeared, and Lisa's face twisted into a sneer.

"You can't tell me what to do anymore!" She confirmed my fears as she looked over at me with a toothy smile.

"You've already downgraded," she said

looking me up and down. I couldn't stop the tears from falling. They fell with the freedom of a child, hot and relentless, dripping down my face and off of my chin. That was the thing I'd discovered about Little Space; the more comfortable I grew with myself and that mindset, the easier I fell into its trap which was that it was hard to pull myself out. I dropped to the floor and cried like an absolute baby even though there were several people watching us at this point, watching me sob.

Lisa gave a girly giggle, sitting back down at the table and picking up her pencil as if nothing had happened. She was blurry through my tears, but I wanted to throw something at her. Before I could, I felt Connor's arms around me. He lifted me up—he carried me around a lot in Little Space—and took me over to the food table.

"Hey," he whispered gently, pressing a kiss to my forehead. He got down on his haunches in front of me, reminding me once again how small I was compared to him, and held my hands.

"This isn't exactly how I pictured your first

play party. There were so many things I wanted to show you. But Daddy will understand completely if you want to leave," he lovingly said. I glanced over my shoulder. That was a mistake. Lisa was watching, and she stuck her tongue out at me like the snake she was. I swiped at tears and whimpered, "I don't think I can stay, Daddy."

"Okay," Connor nodded. I could tell he was disappointed, but he pulled me in and stroked my hair.

"I'm sorry things turned out this way, sweetheart," he gently said, taking my hand in his. With that, Connor led me out of the play party. There were still eyes on us, but I knew what it was like to be a Little. They would all go back to their fun in no time. I might be the talk when they left and went back to their normal lives, but for now, there were more interesting things than the crying girl in overalls. Connor squeezed my hand gently every so often to let me know he was there and when we got into the car, he didn't let go the whole way home.

"I wish I'd gotten a piece of cake," I mumbled sadly, staring out of the window.

***

The following day, as much as I would have liked to stay in bed with Connor's warm arms wrapped around me, I couldn't. But that didn't mean I hopped out of bed, happy to get to my day. My bunny slippers—another gift from Connor— dragged along the floor as I went to get ready. I was lucky enough that Connor was a morning person, which only made me wonder what on earth he was doing with me, as he made coffee and breakfast. How I would have gotten through the day without coffee was beyond me. I certainly hadn't had the time to make it, given the fact that I hit the snooze button on my alarm one too many times.

On the drive to work, I hoped that Lisa wasn't on the same shift as me, mostly because I was wearing a dress. It was the only option at Connor's, but it was less girly than my others; a simple white dress that flared at the waist and ended halfway down my knees, something Connor and I agreed was better for when I wore diapers, which was admittedly quite often. Nevertheless, wearing dresses to work was not something I normally did. My emotions were tangled. Every time I closed my eyes, I could see Lisa's sneer burned into the back of my eyelids. Vulnerability charged through me, and I couldn't help feeling disgusted, as if something were crawling along my skin. Lisa used to be Connor's Little! For a brief moment, I had thought I was special, but I no longer felt that way. Tears threatened to fall again, and I wished that I could call in sick. It wouldn't have been a complete lie. The thought of Lisa and her perfect face, a face I wanted to punch, was enough to make my stomach turn violently.

As much as I wanted to be, I couldn't be mad at Connor. It wasn't as if I'd been a part of his life. I was nothing more than the girl behind the bar. Still, the thought stung. Why did it have to be Lisa? My hope for a quiet morning was dashed as I heard Lisa's greeting chime the moment I sat down in my cubicle. It made me squirm uncomfortably. I glanced out to see her in a dress that showed off all her curves and had a swooping neckline.

I forced myself to look away and focus on my computer screen. There were more important things to do. I wasn't at work for Lisa, after all. And yet, it seemed as if Lisa might be at work for me. She peered over the top of my cubicle, and I knew this wasn't going to be good. Lisa looked like a bitch with unfinished business.

"Isn't it a beautiful day? You should wear dresses more often, Little Jessie. It suits you," Lisa said in the velvet way she spoke. Ignoring her, I opened another email, my heart hammering.

"Little Jessie," she continued, looking around conspiratorially as if we would ever be co-conspirators.

"Are you and your Daddy going to the next play party?" She continued making me want to punch her in the face.

"That's what I thought," Lisa smiled and

walked around, entering my tiny cubicle. I was speechless as she sat back on the limited desk space I had. Her long, tanned legs annoyed me compared to my own short, pale ones.

"I think we can have some fun here. You see, from now on, I'm in charge around here. You're gonna do everything I tell you because if you don't, well, let's just say I'm not so sure I can keep my mouth shut about all the *little* things you've been getting up to lately," she said making me shake my head in despair. The double-meaning didn't escape my notice, and my heart pounded faster than before.

"Why are you doing this, Lisa?" I said, the words coming out more pathetic than I had wished.

"That's not important," she hissed, and for a second, I imagined her as a real snake, flinching.

"Don't even think about saying a word to Connor. If you do, I'll know, and I will make things worse for you," she said as she fidgeted with one of the files on my desk.

"I wonder how the execs would feel about you bringing your private life to work with you," making me blush. My eyes widened.

"What are you talking about?" I said trying to gain some control. Lisa smirked and stretched her leg out to lift the front of my skirt. I pushed back from the desk, escaping her and stood up indignantly. Before I could raise my voice, scream at her like I wanted, she laughed.

"I can see your diaper," Lisa remarked snidely. While I spluttered, heat rushing through my entire body instead of just my cheeks, Lisa shimmied gracefully out of the small space.

Chapter 6

I had the weekend off. It was rare that I had two consecutive days off, much less an entire weekend. Connor took the weekend off because of it, and he was arriving at my house at any moment. I was ready and packed, slumped on my sofa. I had nothing better to do. Normally, I'd have been running around getting things ready at the last minute, but since I'd had such trouble sleeping lately, I'd spent most of the night packing. I'd showered and dressed hours before a text beeped on my phone to let me know that Connor was on the way.

Things with Connor and I had been rocky lately. I got the feeling that he was avoiding me, much to my dismay. One would have thought me being all over him all the time would have been something he enjoyed, but no. Apparently sitting on my knees and waiting for Daddy to get home from work so that I could give him pleasure was cause for concern.

I sighed, rolling my eyes at the memory of Connor's face. I'd expected him to be happy, but he'd gotten down on his knees and asked me if I was okay. Of course, I wasn't okay. Could I tell him that? Of course not.

Perhaps it was the suddenness that got to him. After all, he probably expected me to distance myself after what happened with Lisa. I couldn't though. The only thing that took my mind off of it was Connor and being with Connor. I knew it was wrong, but right now, I didn't know how else to cope.

Things had gotten so much worse at work, and I had no idea what to do anymore. I didn't want to stop being who I was, especially now that I'd figured out who that was, and I still had to follow the rules Connor laid out for me. That meant I was following two different sets of rules because Lisa had a set of her own, designed to torture me. For one thing, Connor's rule was that I wear diapers at all times. How did Lisa counteract this? She wanted me to wear dresses to work at least three times a week. I could be grateful that she didn't make it every day, but I knew she didn't do that for me. I was bound to get strange looks if I walked into the office on the days when we had meetings wearing one of my Little dresses, and it seemed Lisa was having too much fun with me to put a stop to it quite yet.

Outside, I heard Connor's car arrive, followed by the horn. I got up and took my bags with me, heading over to the door. I opened it to find Connor with his hand up, ready to knock on the spot above my head. His mouth dropped open at the sight of me—and my bags.

"This has got to be some kind of miracle. You're actually on time," he said with a smile.

"Well, that's totally uncalled for," I dragged my suitcase behind me, ignoring his offered hand as he tried to take the bag.

"Oh, come on, little one. I was only joking," Connor said, kissing the top of my head. We'd already reached the car, and he popped open the trunk. This time I let him take my suitcase because there was no way I could lift it on my own. My lower lip was pushed out into a pout that I could tell Connor enjoyed far too much.

"You're supposed to comfort me, not look at me like I'm adorable," I said, pouting at him. Connor just grinned.

"But you are adorable," he said, shrugging his shoulders.

"Daddyyy," I whined.

"Okay, okay," he held up his hands in surrender. I knew we were only playing around, but when Connor's eyes crinkled in concern, I wanted to dive under the car and hide away forever.

"Get in the car. We've got to get to the hotel before check-in closes," he said.

"Well, don't look at me. I'm on time," I was already at my door and climbing into the car.

"Watch your attitude, little lady!" Connor called, walking around to the driver's side.

My core tightened at the strict tone of voice. I couldn't help it. Lately, I'd grown more and more bratty. I had a feeling it was the idea of Connor punishing me that did it. As he buckled up and the engine purred to life, I reached into his lap and ran my small hand over the crotch of his jeans.

"Jessie," he murmured warningly. I ignored him, and as we pulled into the road, I unzipped his jeans.

"Jessie, behave yourself," Connor warned.

"Where's the fun in that?" I smirked, reaching in and freeing his cock. It was already hard.

"Besides, you can't exactly say you don't like it," I teased.

"That's beside the point. I'm telling you to behave. If you don't, you're not going to have a very good time on this vacation," he said. I didn't listen to him. My hand was wrapped around his thick shaft, stroking up and down. As angry as he sounded, Connor's breathing had quickened, and his cock was harder than ever. In the hopes that I could assuage him, I leaned across the seat and wrapped my mouth around the tip. It was warm, and I could already taste the precum as I began bobbing my head up and down. There was nothing Connor could do about it—or so I thought. He turned off the next chance he got, pulled over, and turned the engine off. My heart skipped a beat.

"If you don't sit back in your seat and behave, we'll turn around, and you won't see me until next weekend," he said. I immediately pulled off and sat back in my seat, staring at him with wide eyes.

"You wouldn't do that," I gasped.

"Try me," he growled. His jaw was clenched, and I could see a muscle twitching in his cheek. The anger in his eyes was real.

"Rules are rules. And don't think I'm not going to punish you the second we check-in," he sternly said. Swallowing the lump that formed in my throat, I squirmed in my seat.

"Yes, Daddy," I said, my voice came out as barely a whisper. He didn't answer me as he started the car, didn't even look at me as we headed back out onto the road. The rest of the drive was achingly silent. I wanted to put some music on, but I didn't dare move. I'd never seen Connor so angry with me, and I didn't want to push my luck any more than I already had.

***

As soon as we got to the hotel, we changed into our bathing suits. Connor had calmed down immensely, and I was relieved that my butt wouldn't be subject to his wrath. The whole point of the trip was that we could take a special "grown-up" vacation together and we had a couple's massage, facials, and zip-lining on our list of planned activities. I didn't want anything to spoil it.

The only problem was that my phone had vibrated three times since we arrived, and I knew whose messages I'd find if I checked it. It was on silent after the third text from Lisa asking me how my weekend with Daddy was going. My mood was worse than ever. Wasn't it bad enough that she tortured me at work? Did she have to do it on my days off too? What did she even get out of it?

"Jessie?" Connor broke into my thoughts. I looked over at him standing in the doorway of the bathroom, wearing nothing but a towel around his waist, and instantly knew I hadn't been responsive for a while.

"Are you all right, baby girl?" He was clearly concerned.

"I'm fine, Daddy," I said absently.

"You know," he came toward me, and there was a different tone in his voice.

"I think I know something that'll cheer you up," he said. He had that look in his eye again, that hungry one that made me feel like prey, and I could already feel moisture pooling between my legs. I had a tiny pink bikini on, and it couldn't defend against Connor's hands and his mouth. His hand was between my legs, stroking over the bikini bottoms, and his mouth was on my left nipple over the bikini top.
Under his attention, my nipples grew hard, and

goosebumps rose on my skin. Every tiny touch seemed to send a charge of sensation straight to my center, where his fingers were manipulating me in circles. My mouth fell open in a moan as Connor shifted the bathing suit bottoms to the side, giving him full access to my pussy. I knew for a fact that those bottoms had a wet spot on them, but that was irrelevant because all that mattered was that Connor was touching me and my body was singing with pleasure.

Connor broke away from my breasts only to press his lips to mine, eliciting another moan. I kissed him back fervently, but Connor seemed to be playing the slow game. For every advance I made, he took a figurative step back, frustrating me to no end.

"Daddy," I eventually whined, breaking away from his mouth. I reached behind me and pulled on the knot holding my top together, allowing it to fall and leaving my breasts exposed to Connor's eyes, heaving with my breaths.

"I want you..." I said, giving him my best

puppy dog eyes. The towel around his waist had a tent in it, and I reached out to unhook it, revealing Connor's erection. My mouth watered at the sight alone. There was no way he could hide that he wanted me too, so why was he teasing me?

Making love to Connor was the only thing that kept my mind off Lisa. Every other torturous second, I could see her smug face, and it made me angry. I knew I was probably becoming a bit much, but I didn't care. Connor's cock and attention were my distraction, my medicine. I didn't think it was so wrong of me to want my boyfriend as much as I did, especially if it kept me sane.

Connor sensed my urgency. He picked me up so suddenly that I squealed in surprise, promptly giggling as he walked us backward toward the bed. He sat down and positioned me on his lap. Without removing my pink bikini bottoms, Connor lined himself up with my entrance and sat me down on his shaft. We both sighed in pleasure as he filled me up.

I leaned in to kiss him again, whispering against

his lips.

"Thank you, Daddy," I softly said. Normally, that would have been enough to set him off, but not this time. Connor turned into a primal animal whenever I called him Daddy while we had sex. For some reason, today was different.

"Do you know how special you are to me, little one?" He whispered as he began to rock his hips, gliding slowly in and out of me. His fingers were digging into the soft flesh of my butt, aiding him in his thrusts as he lifted and dropped me onto his cock in time with them.

"You mean so much to me," he said looking at me lovingly. My heart hammered in my chest and in spite of myself, my walls clenched and convulsed around his length. With each word he said, I got hotter and hotter. I loved the rough sex and being taken, but this was an entirely new experience, and I didn't know how to react to it. My body, on the other hand, was deeply enjoying itself. I could only moan in response. Tightening my thighs around his waist, I tried to leverage myself to ride him faster and harder, but Connor had a firm grip on me, and he was taking charge. I was close to my orgasm, could feel it building with every delicious stroke of his dick inside me, but I wasn't close enough. I wanted to go over the edge. I wanted the earth to shatter around me. I wanted him to keep moving against that spot until I became a writhing mess.

"Please," I finally whimpered.

"Please fuck me harder, Daddy. Please," I begged. I could see the shock on his face—after all, that should have been grounds for punishment—but Connor didn't stop. He flipped me onto my back beneath his huge muscular body and began driving into me with abandon. I threw my head back and dug my nails into his strong shoulders, my legs open as wide as they could be.

"Is this what you want?" Connor growled down at me.

"You want to be used like a little slut? That's what my little girl wants?" He said, thumping into my pussy.

"Oh, God," I moaned again and again. His words did things to me, and he was hitting that spot every single time he thrust home. I could feel it getting nearer, and I shut my eyes, my breaths coming out in high-pitched whimpers as Connor took me. I could tell he was close too, could feel it in the erratic movements of his hips. And finally, when I felt the heat of him shooting into me, I let go in a loud cry, exploding around him and writhing beneath him.

When Connor finally pulled back from me, he heaved a sigh. I knew he was frustrated—most likely with me—but I didn't know how to help that. This was not the bliss I was used to basking in after Connor took me. I made the mistake of making it worse than it already was by reaching for my phone on the nightstand.

On Monday, I want you to wear the shortest dress you own. I suggest you learn to squat when you need to pick something up. I wouldn't want you to reveal your diaper or anything. You know how clumsy I am.

I huffed and slammed the phone back down on the nightstand. It was all I could do not to throw it across the room. The action caught Connor's notice.

"Jessie, that's it. I'm trying really hard here. I know you need your privacy, but I'm putting my foot down. I want you to tell me what's going on," he said.

"Nothing's going on," I lied, crossing my arms over my chest, fighting while naked brought a whole other level of vulnerability with it.

"I'm serious. Tell me. You know the rules," he said, trying to be patient.

"Fuck the rules!" I cried out. Connor stared at me for a full minute before he pointed to the corner of the room.

"Time out. Stand in the corner," he shouted pointing to the particular corner which took his fancy.

"Oh, so now you wanna punish me?" I spat back, tears hot in my eyes. He gritted his teeth.

"We'll talk when you're ready to tell me

what's really been going on," he said shaking his head.

"That'll be never," I snapped. Nevertheless, I listened to his orders and walked over to the corner with my head down. I stood with my hands behind my back. My throat constricted the way it did when I cried. Disappointing my Daddy wasn't something I ever wanted to do. At that moment, I hated Lisa with every fiber in my body.

Chapter 7

On Monday, I showed up to work wearing the dress Lisa told me to wear. The moment I got to the office, I knew I'd probably made what could be one of the biggest mistakes in my life. Balloons were hanging from the ceiling, a gathering of my colleagues dressed far better than they usually dressed, and tables on tables of food and drink. It was a work function.

The worst part was that I'd known there was a work function coming up, purely because I'd been trying my best to get out of it. Unfortunately, it was compulsory for everyone to attend. The weekend had been so distracting that I completely forgot about the function altogether, forgot about every plan I'd had in place to ensure that Lisa didn't entrap me. Now, I was wearing one of my Little outfits, carrying the bag that I took over to Connor's house when I visited, and a diaper beneath my skirt. Panic struck me, and I immediately made my way toward my cubicle to hide, keeping my head down even as people tried to greet me.

I wished I'd brought Connor along. He was my anchor. I knew if anyone would be able to protect me, it would be him. Honestly, all he had to do was stand beside me, and no one would dare approach the giant, lest he grind their bones for his morning toast or something equally ridiculous. Alas, Connor wasn't here, and I was on my own.

"Well, look at you!" An excited voice suddenly cried out. Lisa raced toward me, wearing a fishtail dress that went all the way down her long legs and made her look more like an hourglass than usual. She looked glamorous and chic, whereas I looked like a cupcake.

"Oh, Little Jessie, I looove that dress on you. We're going to have so much fun!" Lisa said clapping her slender hands together. I wanted to swear at her, but my ass still stung from the weekend. Connor had put me in my place several times while we were at the hotel. I had to admit that eventually, my attitude calmed down, I calmed down, and by the end of the vacation, I was feeling a lot better. The aftercare, being held by my Daddy, turned out to be what I really needed. You know, aside from telling him the truth and letting him give me advice on how to deal with it.

"I take it you kept to our agreement," Lisa said sternly as if she could read my mind. "Connor won't be turning up tonight?" She sneered.

"Connor doesn't know anything about how horrible you are if that's what you're asking, Lisa," I said. She gave a giggle, girlish and falsely sincere.

"Good. That's the way I like it. Now run along and get coffee for me, will you? You know how I like it," she simply said. With that, she rejoined the party on the other side of the office, sashaying in between a group of men and dancing to the music as it played. All eyes were on her, including mine. I made my way toward the kitchen and made her a cup of coffee, exactly the way she liked it. Lisa had some kind of magical extra sense that made it impossible to spike her drink or even spit in it. She would know. I already tried.

The sound of the kettle boiling helped. It was white noise, blocking out the sounds of the function. In all honesty, even if Lisa wasn't torturing and blackmailing me, I wouldn't have enjoyed the function. I never had before. The firm wasn't exactly my idea of fun. It was stifling, and it blocked any sense of creativity I might have had. It's probably why my favorite pastime as a Little was to color. I'd always loved art.

With a click of the kettle, I poured the water into Lisa's special cup, a cup no one in the office ever drank from if they wanted to keep their jobs and added some creamer before reluctantly rejoining the function.

Lisa was easy enough to spot. All one had to do was look for the group of men huddled in one particular area. She'd be in the middle of them, showered with the attention of men who all wanted to sleep with her. I didn't know why they bothered. It was obvious to me that she would never give them the time of day.

"Here you go, Lisa," I called, making my way through the gap. This was one of Lisa's rules. No matter what she was doing, I was to follow through on what she'd asked me to do. It was her way of making sure I got the attention I desperately wanted to avoid.

"Your coffee," I meekly said. I froze in my tracks when I saw Lisa. She had my backpack strapped to her shoulders; the overnight bag I was meant to be taking to Connor's later that night. The men were all chuckling as she twirled round and round with it, making fun of its rainbow colors. My breath hitched.

"What are you doing?" I demanded.

"Oh, there you are, Little Jessie!" Lisa clapped her hands.

"I was just showing off your bag. The boys think that I should have it. Don't you, boys?" She said with her snake eyes looking at me.

"Hear, hear!" The cry was accompanied by

the scent of alcohol. The men had been drinking punch for quite some time.

"That's not funny," I said, moving deeper into the huddle.

"Give it back," I added quickly.

"But I don't want to," Lisa hissed.

"I don't care what you want, Lisa! It's my bag," I yelled. I could feel my blood being to boil. Lisa's eyes darkened, the blue flashing as she glared at me.

"Is that so? Well, Jessie, I want you to back down. This is my bag now," she teased.

"No, Lisa, it isn't," I said glaring at her. The men were no longer laughing, but the stupid pop songs that Lisa loved to listen to were still playing in the background. I knew she was in charge of the playlist because I could hear this very same playlist coming from her earphones whenever she left work early. They were songs that I might have liked if not for their connection to Lisa. As it was, they only added fuel to the fiery rage I felt simmering within me.

There was no mistaking the look in Lisa's eyes. She wanted me to back down, wanted me to submit to her will as I had been, but I was too angry. Lisa had finally crossed a line. If it weren't for her, nothing would be wrong in my relationship, and I was tired of feeling so worn down. If it weren't for her, I would have had a better weekend, one without tears. If it weren't for her, my experiences as a Little would have been a hundred times better. I tried to figure out what would happen if I didn't back down. What could Lisa do? It wasn't as if she could simply out me. Most people didn't even understand what a Little or a Daddy Dom was. I would know since I'd been a part of that majority several months ago.

"Are you sure you wanna do this?" Lisa asked, arching one of her perfect brows at me the way she always did when she was testing my will.

"Give me my bag," I said, this time, I wasn't going to break.

Lisa's face broke into a grin that made my heart skip a beat.

"Don't say I didn't warn you," Lisa said shrugging her shoulders. In one swift move, Lisa ripped my backpack off her shoulders and unzipped the top compartment.

"No!" I screamed, diving for her.

The coffee landed on the floor, hot and steaming. Men jumped away from us as I knocked Lisa to the ground, reaching for my bag. Lisa managed to hold it out of my reach until I grabbed a handful of her long blonde hair, recalling the way she'd tugged at my pigtails at the play party. She grunted in pain and knocked her elbow back, hitting me right beneath my ribs. The sting and force threw both the breath and the strength out of me.

"Stop it!" Someone cried out.

"What the hell is going on here?" Another added. We didn't hear them. We were too occupied with our fight for my backpack. Despite their protests, no one intervened.

Lisa took the opportunity to push me off onto my back on the ground. One hand clutched my side as I tried to catch my breath, and that's when she took her chance. I could only watch on in horror, crying out for her to stop. Lisa turned my backpack upside down and began shaking it until one by one. The contents fell onto the ground.

The first thing to fall was a notebook and pen, the second thing a packet of coloring pencils, and that was followed by my coloring book. If that wasn't bad enough, I already knew what was coming next. I knew Lisa wouldn't stop until every last item was out for everyone to see. She giggled and laughed so hard that mascara streaks ran down her high cheekbones. I stood from the ground, wishing I could kick her in the face, in the same second that one of my adult diapers and a pink paci landed on the floor of the office.

I shouldn't have even bothered trying to cover it up, but that didn't stop me from diving for it. Lisa's malicious laugh rang out above me, and once she started laughing, everyone started laughing. That's when I realized my skirt had lifted in the fight. It didn't matter that I tried to cover up the coloring book, paci, or diaper. Everyone had already seen mine, covered in tiny stickers of butterflies that Connor had bought for me to make them prettier.

"Oh, my God. This is even better than I imagined it would be," Lisa said through laughter. Maybe if I didn't have people laughing at me from every direction, I might have stood up and punched her.

Instead, I gathered all my things and shoved them back into my bag as quickly as I could. I didn't even bother zipping it up before I hightailed it out of there. The sound of laughter followed me all the way into my car, echoing in my ears as I started the engine and made my way home.

***

Tears rolled down my cheeks as I answered the phone.

"Jessie? Are you still at work?" His voice was like butter.

"No, I'm not," I sobbed.

"What happened? What's going on? Are you okay?" He said, as he bombarded me with questions before I had the chance to answer, not that I knew how to answer. For a second, I forgot he couldn't see me shaking my head on the other side of the phone. I pulled the covers over my body, hiding from the world.

"Jessie, please talk to me. Please," he said, concern in his voice.

"Lisa emptied my bag in front of everyone at work. They all saw my diaper and other stuff," I cried.

"She did *what*. That fucking—"?!" Connor yelled, making me flinch.

"I'm fine," I interrupted.

"Do you want me to come over? I can bring food. And a movie," he said. I loved that he was trying.

"No, please don't. Don't come over. Not tonight," I said, deciding it was better to be alone.

"Jessie..." His voice was low, and I could almost see him running his hands through his hair.

"Please. I want to be alone. I just want to be alone," I said. He sighed, blowing static into my ear. When he spoke again, the anger had all but gone. His voice was gentle.

"I'll be here when you're ready to come back to me, baby girl," he said before hanging up the phone.

Chapter 8

I'd long since succumbed to the numbness that echoed throughout every part of my body. I couldn't feel anything. I lay in bed, lifeless, and disconnected from the world. It was a world I wanted nothing to do with anyway. It was cruel, and so were the people in it.

Lisa was the one who broke me and ruined my life, but somehow, I couldn't stop thinking about all the people in the world who were exactly like her. There were so many, and in the terrible state of mind I found myself in, I lingered on them. Needless to say, it didn't exactly improve my mood or state of mind. On the contrary, I sank into a pit of despair where I wondered what exactly the point of ever leaving the house again would be.

I hadn't been back to work since Lisa exposed me in front of all those people. The memory of their faces, all of my colleague's judgmental faces, was enough of a deterrent. Alongside my fear that they might look at me that way again, might never stop looking at me that way, it was the thought that they could do worse things that kept me at bay. After all, there was no telling how many of them were like Lisa. If she could empty my bag out like that, who was to say others wouldn't behave the same way?

I wasn't sure how long it had been since the event, but I wouldn't have been surprised if several days had passed. It felt as though I'd been drowning in my shame for years. Nevertheless, I'd begun to think about what I could be missing. Withdrawing from the world that hurt me seemed like a good idea at the time. Unfortunately, I knew that I would have to emerge from my blankets eventually.

Connor invaded my thoughts. I couldn't stop thinking about how angry he'd been the last time he called. The anger hadn't been directed at me, and though I didn't think it at the time, it was kind of sweet how he wanted to stand up for me.

At the thought of climbing out of bed, every single bone in my body ached, but I knew I had to do it. I'd made up my mind. I could only stand to wallow in my own self-pity for so long. I threw the duvet off of me as if ripping a bandage off of a fresh wound.

Somehow, I immediately felt better. I didn't realize how hot I was until I felt the cool air on my legs.

I decided to take small, slow steps, treating myself as I would a scared, rescued kitten beginning to trust the world again. If I moved too quickly, took in too much, I might run back to my hiding place. I calmly sat myself up, and one by one swung my legs to the side of the bed. I sat there for a moment, taking in deep slow breaths.

My chest was tight and sore. It felt like this was the first time I was breathing since my withdrawal, and only now did I realize how thick and stuffy the air in my room actually was. I needed to open the windows or something, along with change the sheets. It was dark and stuffy in my room. I think I closed the curtains the day I got home from the function, and they'd been closed since.

I knew that I'd been dramatic over the past several days, but I felt like I had the right to be, given the circumstances.

Forcing myself to stand up, I made my way over to the curtains. My hands moved mechanically, flinging the curtains open before I had the chance to rethink my decision. I narrowed my eyes and prepared to be blinded by the bright sunlight flooding into my room. That didn't happen. It was actually grey and cloudy outside. A short snort escaped as I considered the fact that the world was sulking along with me.

Opening the windows and breathing in the wonderful smell of rain to come, I felt just a tiny bit better than before, despite having felt as though I would never feel good again only moments before. The only things left to do were brush my teeth, wash my body, and try to get rid of the smell stinking up my room. Part of me thought that smell might just be me.

I wasn't ready to rejoin the world, but a shower was well overdue. My phone rang as I made my way to the bathroom, and I paused for a moment, thinking about answering it. My phone had been ringing non-stop since the function. I was worried that if I picked it up, it would be someone I didn't want to talk to. The mere thought of seeing a name I didn't want to see kept me away.

More than anything, I thought if it was Connor, I wouldn't be able to ignore it. Not knowing who was calling or why was the safest option. So, naturally, I decided to ignore it again.

My phone rang several more times while I was in the shower, but I was too busy enjoying the hot water cascading down my skin, and the smell of fruity scents of my body wash and shampoo. I didn't care if it was ringing or not.

Once my body was clean, I simply stood beneath the running water and breathed in the steam. It was amazing how therapeutic showers could be. People often overlooked that, myself included. Then again, it wasn't as if I could spend all day in a shower. Otherwise, that's probably how my last few days would have played out, rather than reducing myself to the lump under the bed covers.

Eventually, I jumped out of the shower. Getting dried and dressed was relatively easy, apart from the fact that my muscles ached with lack of use. I thought I might have wanted to jump right back into bed but seeing at how dirty and messed up it looked made me want to throw it all in the wash instead. I walked past my phone on the way to the washing machine and heard a single message tone go off.

It made me pause for a moment. Answering a phone call was something I was completely against at this stage, but how bad could looking at a message be? Odds were there were several waiting for me. If it was from Connor, I might be inclined to answer him, but at least I wouldn't have to talk to him. I didn't think I could handle hearing his voice yet. The anger I'd heard still haunted me.

In the end, my curiosity got the better of me, and I

looked at my phone.

It was an email, which wasn't Connor's style. If not Connor, who could it be? I ignored all the missed call notifications and went straight to the email. It was from the law firm, and it was a rather lengthy text, but my eyes zoomed in on one particular sentence.

We regret to inform you that your employment with us is hereby terminated.

My mouth fell open as I skimmed through the rest of the email.

Having tried and failed to get a hold of you several times over the past few days for a hearing with the firm, we have accepted that you are not interested in explaining yourself. After a thorough investigation into the events of the last function, we would have liked to give you a chance. However, your absence and silence are unacceptable, and we can no longer wait for you to return to the office.

I gulped the emotional lump that formed in my throat and scanned the missed call notifications. It turned out Connor hadn't been calling me, after all.

They were all from the law firm.

My phone clattered to the floor shortly before I did, falling to my knees. If not for the soft, plush carpet, I might have hurt myself. As it was, I bent my head forward into my hands to stop the world from spinning around me. Bile threatened to rise in my throat, and I moved my arms to clutch my stomach instead.

How could I lose my job? I can't have lost my job.

With my thoughts all over the place, I didn't have the slightest inkling of what to do. There was only one constant; Connor. Somehow, I knew that Connor would know what to do. He would know how to help because, of course, he always did. He was always there when I needed him, always there to take care of me, and always a soothing balm to everything I dealt with. It had been that way long before we ever entered into our contract together. Despite everything, I knew that he cared about me. It wasn't lack of care that kept his name out of my notifications. On the contrary, it was the complete opposite. I'd asked him to give me space, and he'd respected my wishes.

And suddenly, I knew without complete and utter clarity that I needed him.

Once the thought entered my mind, I was like a woman possessed and no longer in control of the reins. I grabbed my keys, locked my place up, made a beeline for my car, and raced toward Connor's house. It was like someone else was moving my feet. Someone else lifted my hand. Someone else knocked on Connor's front door. Honestly, I could hardly remember how I got there at all. I was consumed by one thought, and one thought only.

I need my Daddy.

When the door finally opened, and I saw Connor's familiar strong features and his startling blue eyes, something inside me broke. It finally collapsed under the immense weight I'd been carrying for so long. The tears pricked and built up in my eyes, and I fell right into his arms.

I'd prepared to be rejected and to have the door

slammed in my face. Connor would have been well within his rights to push me away, but he didn't. Instead, he held his arms open, and when I fell into them, he wrapped his arms around me tightly, holding me to his chest. The calm and steady sound of his heartbeat lulled me, and soon, my breathing and heart rate slowed to match up to his.

As if nothing ever happened between us, as if I'd seen him only the day before, he pulled me inside and closed the door behind us.

***

Connor took me inside, and we sat down in his living room.

"Are you ready to talk to me, baby girl?" His voice was gentle as if he were worried, I might break. I suppose I couldn't blame him. Tears were rolling down my cheeks.

"I got fired from the law firm this morning," I managed to mumble through sobs.

"It was all Lisa. She was the reason I couldn't talk to you. She told me that if I did that, she would know and make it worse for me," I explained.

"Lisa threatened to tell everyone about us, didn't she?" He was still gentle, but I could tell from the tightness of Connor's jaw that he was clenching his teeth.

"What did she have you do?" He asked. I sighed heavily.

"It was stupid, really. I basically had to act like her unpaid intern, get coffee for her, and act as if she were my boss. That sort of thing. It wouldn't have been so bad if not for the fact that I hated my job already and Lisa is a total bitch," I said. Connor flinched at the swear word, but I continued.

"You should have seen their faces, Daddy," I breathed out.

"Fuck them," Connor suddenly said. This time it was my turn to flinch, and I stared at him with wide eyes.

"I mean it. You don't need them. They're idiots and anyway, if you think about it, now you're finally free of them," he said.

"What do you mean?" I sniffed. Before he responded, Connor stood and got a box of tissues from the other side of the room. He pulled one out and, instead of handing it to me, got down on his haunches in front of me and began wiping gently at my eyes and nose. While he cleaned me up, he continued.

"You hated that job, baby girl. It didn't suit you. The people were horrible, and the environment was stifling," he said. When he was done, he gave me a small smile. My eyes were still watery but no longer pouring.

"Think about it this way; you have the chance to spread your wings and do something you actually enjoy now," he continued.

"I guess," I mumbled. I wasn't quite sold on the idea, but he was right about one thing. Losing my job wasn't so bad, and I was kind of relieved that I'd never have to go back into the office again.

"You know, even through all this, I never stopped thinking about you. I'm sorry I hung up on you. I know now that I need you in my life," I said.

Connor pressed the tip of his index finger against my lips.

"Shhh, it's okay. All is forgiven. Let Daddy take care of you," Connor said. Nodding my head, I submitted. At Connor's gentle guidance, I laid down on the couch, and he pressed a kiss to my forehead before disappeared into the kitchen. The sound of utensils and cutlery could be heard as he cooked, lulling me to sleep. After everything, I suddenly felt eerily calm, and I knew it was because of my Daddy.

When I woke from my nap, it was to the delicious smell of chicken soup. Connor had reappeared, and he took me into his arms, sitting me up as I came to. A bowl sat on the table, alongside a spoon. The moment I reached for them, however, Connor held me back.

"No, no," he murmured. I relaxed against his arms, gladly resting against his chest as he put a bib around my neck.

"I'm feeding you, little one," he said. Heat rushed to my cheeks as Connor grabbed the bowl whilst holding me in both arms. Slowly, he carried spoonful after spoonful into my mouth. The soup tasted even better than it smelled, and it warmed my body as it traveled down my throat. Once or twice, it spilled onto my chin and Connor would simply use the bib to wipe it off.

I wasn't sure I'd ever felt as at peace as I did at that moment. Little Space felt more like a home than anywhere else, especially when I was in my Daddy's arms, and although we'd practiced the kink for a while now, I wasn't sure I fully understood why Littles were so happy until this moment. It was as if I could melt into his arms and stay there forever.

Soon, however, the bowl was empty, and I was full. Connor set it down on the table, and we simply sat there for a while. He ran his fingers softly through my hair and rocked back and forth, threatening to make me fall asleep once again. For this moment, I was able to forget about everything.

That was until Connor slipped out from behind me and stood up. Before I could say or ask anything though, he slid his one arm behind the small of my back and the other arm beneath my knees. He picked me up as if I weighed nothing and carried me to the bathroom. I allowed myself to relax as Connor undressed me and ran me a nice hot bath. I thought it best not to mention that I already had a shower before I drove to his place. I wanted him to take care of me and the bubble bath, looked so good. Thus, I simply kept quiet and enjoyed the caregiving I was receiving.

Once the bath was full and Connor had checked the temperature of the water, he picked me up and lowered me into it. As sleepy as I was, I simply sank into the bubbles and sighed as their silkiness brushed across my skin. The next thing I knew, Connor grabbed a loofa and poured way too much body wash into it before washing my body. He treated me as if I were a fragile thing that might break at any minute, grazing the sponge along my back and down my legs with slow and methodical motions.

It can't get any better than this.

I was convinced that Connor was washing away every single worry and care that plagued my existence, and I hummed with pleasure. This earned me another kiss on the forehead. For the first time in days, I smiled up at Connor.

"Is my little girl enjoying bath time?" He asked.

"Yes, Daddy. Thank you," I whispered.

"It's always a pleasure to take care of my baby girl," he said. Next, Connor washed my hair, and his fingers massaging my scalp felt so good that my eyes rolled back. All too soon, I was clean—thoroughly if one considered the shower I'd had beforehand—and Connor emptied the bathtub. He wrapped me up in a towel and once again lifted me up like I was nothing.

"You're like a mountain," I mumbled absent-mindedly, wrapping my arms around his shoulders. Connor grinned down at me.

"And what does that make you?" He asked.

"I don't know. I'm a leaf or something," I said.

"A leaf?" He asked, incredulously. Connor's laugh was booming, echoing down the hallway and rumbling through his huge body.

"I think you're more like a butterfly or a cute little bird," he said. I pouted. My voice came out husky with sleep since I was already halfway into dreamland.

"A butterfly?" I asked.

"Mhmm," he hummed as we entered the bedroom.

"Because you're beautiful and full of color," he explained.

"Oh," I couldn't think of anything else to say, but I couldn't resist smiling at the thought of Connor thinking I was beautiful and full of color.

"See, beautiful," he nodded. The bed gave way beneath my tired body, and I got comfortable immediately as Connor set me down, but then he turned away and began to walk out of the room.

"Wait! Where are you going?" I called. I was rewarded with that look that he gave me, the one where his dimples appeared even though he wasn't smiling.

"I'll be right back, little one," he lovingly said.

"Oh," I settled back down. I needn't have worried because he wasn't away for too long and when he came back, it was with a blanket, a pacifier, and my favorite stuffie Peanut Butter. Surprised by how much joy I felt, I tried to conceal it even though I wanted to dance and giggle with giddiness. Connor took his place beside me and threw the blanket over us. His huge arms engulfed me next, and I was only too happy to settle against his chest. I looked up at him, my mouth open, and he slid the paci in. I bit down on it and sucked it gently as Connor passed me my stuffie. Content as could be, I let my heavy eyelids fall shut as I squeezed it tightly in my arms.

The slight rise and fall of Connor's chest as he took deep breaths in and out lulled me to sleep. Everything that had happened between us, at work, and in my room faded away. There was no thought, sound, or situation that could pull me from this contentedness. I thought that if it was like this for the rest of my life, then I wouldn't have minded in the slightest.

My Daddy knew exactly how to take care of me.

Chapter 9

The following morning brought trepidation and the familiar feelings I'd been wallowing in. Rather than feel the warm glow of happiness I'd basked in the previous evening, I was struck once more with the reminders of the awful past few days. I hated my memory instantly, wishing it were bad enough to let me be in peace at least for the first minutes of the day.

The curtains were open, and sunshine broke into the room in a thousand blinding rays. The first light of dawn caused me to pull the blanket over my head and shut my eyes tighter than ever. It didn't really do me any good. Sleep had already forsaken me, and I knew it was too late to slip back into the realm of dreams. Still, that didn't stop me from trying.

"Come on, baby girl," Connor's voice broke through the cover of my blanket, and I had to resist the urge to sigh.

What was the point? The world was much safer here in the safety of bed. I pulled the blankets around my shoulders tighter and turned over into the warmth of the bedsheets beneath me. As much as I didn't want to ignore Connor, there was something that just pulled me back into myself. My limbs felt slow and heavy, as if I was pressed into the mattress by some invisible force that insisted on keeping me there.

"Jessie," I heard Connor sigh before feeling the mattress dip under his weight behind me. He settled in next to me, and his hand landed on my shoulder gently, not saying anything for a few minutes as we laid there.

What was wrong? Was he not going to say or do anything? I was sure that he was going to punish me for not listening the first time, but he seemed rather resigned at this point.

It couldn't have been because of last night, could it? No, that wasn't it. Things were back to normal between the two of us when I came over, especially after apologizing for keeping everything involving Lisa from him. Besides, the man who cared for me and said all was forgiven didn't seem like a man who would switch back to being upset with me, if I thought about it. No, last night was filled with love.

I knew that one night was not enough to fix my entire life, but I had hoped that it would solve at least this part, this slice of heaven where I could feel safe and be myself again.

"Jessie," he tried again. I pulled the blanket down and turned my head up at him, taking in his warm hand, still resting over my shoulder.

"Are you okay, sweetheart?" He asked. If I had to be honest, I wasn't sure about how to express how I felt. One part of me was glad to be rid of that witch, realizing that Connor truly had been right about the people at my office being horrible, but another missed my job. It was familiar. There were always ups and downs that came with it, but I did like having some kind of routine. If nothing else, it was a reason to get out of bed. It was something that was mine. More than anything else, it certainly was a way of paying my bills. I had no idea how I was going to do that now.

"I'll be okay," was probably the most honest answer I could have given him. Finally, I rolled over to face that patient smile that made my insides melt. He leaned down and placed a reassuring kiss on my lips—nothing more than a feather-light brush—and rose to his feet, making my cheeks burn before the blankets around me were ripped away.

"Daddy!" I complained before rushing at them, trying to pull them back to the bed but Connor's grip held them far out of my reach, giant that he was.

He wasn't going to let it be that easily with that annoyingly sexy grin of his. If he wanted to play tug-of-war, he could bring it on. It wasn't a fair fight. Connor was bigger and stronger than I was. His hands practically covered half the material whereas mine only gripped at one small corner. That didn't stop me from trying though—at least until I lost my grip and went flying off the side of the bed with a cry of terror.

Connor didn't let me fall. The blanket was abandoned, dropped onto the floor, and I fell into his waiting arms. The force of momentum pushed us both to the floor, and I couldn't help but pout at having lost the battle. Connor, on the other hand, chuckled deeply as he held me close.

"You know, I could always climb back into bed without the blanket. It's totally still an option," I said. I let out a huff and got a light spank on my ass that made me flinch in response.

"Either you come out on your own, or I carry you down for breakfast. You know the rules," he chastised.

"Can I have it in bed today?" I asked.

"I think you've spent quite enough time in bed. At some point you'll have to remember what the rest of your apartment looks like, you know," he shook his head.

"Except this isn't *my* apartment," I pointed out.

"It'll be good practice for you," he answered sternly, never missing a beat. My lips pressed together. As much as I was ready to argue that there was no forgetting my apartment, I knew he was right. I didn't want to admit how often I'd taken my food back to bed on the odd occasion that I did happen to get out of it.

"Yes, Daddy," I said. I walked behind him as we went to the kitchen where breakfast was already on the table. I had to admit it looked good. Plates filled with fluffy scrambled eggs and a couple of streaks of bacon sitting next to them waited for us. A separate plate with golden slices of toast looked too good to describe.

My stomach let out an appreciative grumble as we sat down, and the smell hit my nose. Connor let out a low chuckle. My cheeks warmed at the realization that my belly grumbled loud enough for him to hear it.

"Do you want me to heat it up again or would you rather not want to wait?" He asked. Before I could say anything, my stomach answered for me, making him laugh again.

"Well, that answers that. Go ahead and eat. I'll join you in a second," he laughed. There was something intimate about watching Connor moving around the kitchen as I ate at the table. It wasn't the first time, but there were times where I had been too wrapped up in Little mode to pay attention to these moments, moments when I realized just how attractive my *boyfriend* really was—my belly bubbled with giddiness that came out in a giggle that caused Connor to glance over his shoulder in silent question. I took in things like the way the hem of his shirt lifted when he reached for the coffee on the top shelf or how his hair seemed to reflect the light in just the right way, making the color more intense than I'd ever seen it before.

It was then that I realized it; I loved this man. The words flowed through me with every quickened heartbeat, getting stronger the longer my eyes stayed locked on him, even when he smiled upon catching me staring at him. That look took my breath away. I could have sworn that my inner self was ready to burst into flames once again, warmed by the sudden shock that I'd found the person I wanted to be with always as well as the fact that I was a completely different person from the one who walked into the bar to complain about work only a short while ago.

"Jessie don't play with your food," Connor's voice echoed in my little bubble as he sat down with his own plate in front of him, bringing me back from my daydream.

"Sorry, Daddy," I murmured, shifting. I looked down at my hands to see that I'd been pushing around the last bit of my eggs. Did I really eat everything and not realize it? I guess I really *was* hungry. I settled back to my eggs, grabbing a slice of toast to scoop the remainder onto as Connor sipped his coffee. We ate in silence for a few moments before Connor cleared his throat.

"The past few days haven't been easy for you. And as much as you'll probably want to argue with me, I'm concerned about you, especially with regards to what you're going to do with your life now," he started. The thoughts had crossed my mind. Of course, they had. I was especially concerned about the apartment. It was almost the end of the month and even if they were willing to give me the last month's rent, how was I going to afford the next month? What about the student loans that I still had to pay off or even food? Things weren't exactly cheap these days, and even though I had some money in my savings account, that wasn't going to last for very long. My boss may have been a hotshot lawyer, but that didn't mean he paid much.

The idea of finding another job, however, made my stomach twist. I was never good at that part. I recalled an embarrassing moment when I'd applied to a fast food restaurant to earn some extra cash while I was studying—the manager thought I was asking him on a date and I walked away with his number on the back of a napkin, alongside a sly wink as he passed me a handful of free packets of sauce.

"Jessie, listen to me for a sec before those wheels go taking you far away again. I didn't mean to send you on a thought tangent, but there was something I wanted to say. As much as you were attached to your job at that company, I don't think that going back would be the best idea. Especially with that woman still there," Connor continued as those eyes of his observed her over his coffee mug. It was true. Even if I did go back, there was no guarantee that Lisa wasn't going to start trouble again. Not to mention that there were other people in the company who knew my secret and chances were that many of them wouldn't let me forget about it that easily. If I had learned anything in my lifetime, it was that humans were unnecessarily cruel to each other. That and people who were different or unusual got it even worse than the rest.

"What am I supposed to do then, Daddy?" I asked quietly. Connor's gaze softened at my question. It must have come out a little more childlike than either of us expected from me lately, but that was what he was there for. He was my guide, among other things, and no one could put me at ease like he could.

"Well, picking yourself up and trying again is step one. I'll help you look for a new job if you want me to, but you're a big girl and being able to start over after something like this shows me that. Things will be better when you find a place where you actually fit in. Even though you're still my little girl and I'll be there for you as much as you need, you still have responsibilities outside of us." he said, putting down his mug and took one of my hands in between his bigger ones as he looked into my eyes.

I nodded before I felt warm, wet tears trickling down my face as my free hand closed around the fabric of my pajamas as if the motion itself was going to hold myself together. Why? Why were those words enough to make me cry? Before all of this, the idea of starting over seemed a pleasant one, but there was something about this situation that struck somewhere in the middle of my chest. I didn't quite know where the tears were coming from, only that they wouldn't stop.

Connor hooked his other arm around my waist and pulled me to him, positioning me on his lap with my head nestled in the crook of his shoulder before I had the chance to realize what was happening. It must be fun being a giant; they get huge things done in tiny amounts of time. His hand rubbed my back gently as I breathed in his familiar scent, both setting me at ease.

"Remember, you don't have to hold yourself back in front of me," he murmured. So, I did. The stress of everything that had been happening welled up inside of me, coming out once again as I relished in the comfort and safety of Connor's embrace. I could stay in his arms always. No matter how many times the thought occurred to me, I didn't think I would ever stop being amazed at how much better having a Daddy like Connor made me feel about myself and my life.

Although I have to admit, I didn't remember when I'd become such a cry baby. By the time I stopped sobbing long enough to wipe my tears, I was sure that Connor's legs had fallen asleep with the dining chair beneath the two of us. He didn't let on that he was the slightest bit uncomfortable, which only made me happier.

"Are you feeling better, sweetheart?" He finally asked me. And I was sure that for the first time in days, I was.

***

"I had an idea that I wanted to bring up with you during breakfast," Connor told me while helping me make the bed. Connor was supposed to head to work soon, but he decided to call in to say that he was running late due to an emergency. It was sweet to think that he would do that to make sure that I was okay even though I told him that he didn't need to.

"I suppose now is as good a time as any. What would you say about us living together?" he asked. All at once, I'd transformed into a bundle of nerves, set off by his words, barely managing to contain myself. I tucked in the sheet and set up the pillows, placing Peanut Butter right in front. He looked like such a happy little bear, and I smiled as I turned to Connor and tried my best to keep my voice even.

"What do you mean? Like, me moving in with you?" I questioned wanting clarification.
He nodded.
"It would be temporary, but yes. At least so you can save some money until you find another job. I mean, you spend a lot of time here anyway. This way, you wouldn't have to worry about some things," he explained.

"Okay," I said in a small voice, I didn't have to think about it for very long, this was an easy decision.

***

With Connor's help, it took another week or so for me to pack up my apartment. My furniture and some of the larger things were moved into storage while my clothes and the smaller things like the stuffed animals that he'd given me accompanied me to his apartment. There were so many grown-up actions that needed to be done, responsibilities that simply had to be seen to. Thankfully, my landlords were understanding about my moving out on short notice. They had given me extra time to pay off the lease cancellation fees and the last month's rent. Hopefully, I would find a way to make some money before then.

I was on my own for the drive there, and my stomach had a knot sitting in the middle of it. It was a really big change compared to going to Connor's—no, *our*—apartment before this. There used to be just a simple overnight bag that I kept in case I went over to his for a play session, but now.

Now there was no need for that. We'd be living together.

The thought both made me excited and nervous. I knew that I'd be seeing other sides of Connor now, sides I'd never seen before. There were things that one only found out about another person upon living with them. How did he keep the bathroom? Did he actually do dishes even when he wasn't expecting company? Were the cushions on the sofa always fluffed? This was going to be a learning experience and a half, for both of us.

When I got to the apartment, I was grateful that Connor had already had the good sense to remember to give me a key to let myself in while he was out—something I'd never have remembered on my own. It was much neater than I remember it being the last time I was there, not that it wasn't neat the last time, but I could swear even the scent had changed. There was that familiar scent of lemons that came with most generic cleaning supplies.

A jangle of keys sounded from the other side of the front door, and it opened to reveal Connor holding a covered box in his hands. My brows knitted together as he carried it over to the table and set it down, smiling at me in that way he did when he gave me presents.

"Hey, baby girl, all settled in?" He asked as he came over and gave me an affectionate kiss on the forehead. Before he could move away, my hands caught his waist and pulled him back for a proper one, tilting my head all the way back to meet his towering form. He pulled away with a sexy chuckle and gestured toward the box. Tugging my lower lip between my teeth, I ventured over to the table, raising the cover off the box and staring up at me with dark chocolate eyes cuter than buttons was a small white bunny rabbit. Its clean, white fur looked softer than anything I had ever touched before. It was so tiny with a twitching nose, and its beady eyes never moved from me, looking up with curiosity. When I reached out to give it a pet, I was excited to find out that I was right. My heart was warm, and I was beaming with pure happiness. It was like touching a cloud.

"I can see you love her already," Connor rubbed my back gently as I pet the bunny. I looked at the little fluff ball, and my heart melted as, under my gentle pets, it decided to curl up to go to sleep on the small blanket that was in the corner of the box.

"Thank you so much for the gift, Daddy!" I squealed. He just laughed, looking rather pleased with himself for the choice of gift.

"Would you like to go shopping for supplies for her later? She'll need a proper hutch we can put in the garden and food if we're going to keep her," Connor explained. I nodded enthusiastically, simply eager to both spend any time with him, as well as provide some comfort for our new family member.

"Have you thought of a name for her yet?" Connor asked.

"I'll call her Cloud," I giggled as I kissed her head.

Chapter 10

"Are you ready for this?" Connor asked. We were sitting on the plush carpet—my choice—in his living room. I was happily curled up in his arms, doodling in a notebook, while he worked on our brand-new contract. It seemed he was finally done because the sound of his fingers flying across the keyboard had ceased, and he was pressing soft kisses to the curve between my neck and shoulder, making me giggle like a little girl.

"Daddy! That tickles!" I exclaimed.

"C'mon, Jessie, I can't read it without you," Connor said.

"Okay, okay," I said, I knew what my name meant in this particular case. I put my notebook down and sat up straighter. Since I lost my job, it was rare to find me out of Little Space. He turned the screen for me to look at the document he'd spent days typing up for us, taking in every tiny consideration.

"Is it all done? This is our new contract?" I asked.

"It is indeed," Connor replied. I began reading through our new terms. Connor told me that we had to reevaluate since I was living with him now. Based on the fact that our dynamic had changed, it made sense. All of the previous rules and agreements were still there. Neither of us had issues with the things we'd tried so far. There were simply a number of additions to be made.

Be waiting for Daddy after his shift. That one made me light up.

"It's totally the best way to wind down after work," I grinned at Connor.

"I can't argue with you there," he said.

Take care of Cloud during the day. This one needn't have been added. I adored my rabbit and feeding, bathing, and playing with her gave me great joy. I even enjoyed cleaning her cage because she would twitch her little nose and hop over to me to check out what I was doing every time. Still, it made me feel better to know I had daily responsibilities.

Do your chores. Connor helped me make the bed in the mornings, but I still had to do laundry and clean up after myself.

No dessert before dinner. I flushed. It was only one time, one occasion where Connor had gotten home earlier than expected to find me eating ice cream before dinner. I'd been punished for the simple fact that I looked guilty enough to know I shouldn't have been doing it.

Bathe in the evening with Daddy. I pressed my thighs together at the thought. It turned out Connor quite liked it when I washed his back. I'd done it once, and now it was a rule.

Some of the other rules were ones that were pretty obvious but needed to be written down, just in case I decided to be bratty according to Connor. His logic was that I might be deterred if I knew punishment was a consequence. Most of the time, this was true. My nature couldn't be helped, though. There were times where I found myself giving Connor attitude without even meaning to.

Don't backtalk.

Don't swear.

Don't lie.

Don't steal.

Don't break things.

Do art at least once a day. That was one we hadn't discussed before.

"Once a day?" I asked.

"Mhmm. You're an incredibly talented artist, Jessie. I don't want you squandering it. Plus, I love it when you paint and draw things for me," Connor said.

"You really love it?" I asked. Connor pulled me in and pressed a kiss to the top of my head.

"Of course, I do, sweetheart. I'm not just saying that. You have some serious skills, especially considering you've never taken classes," he said. Smiling, I returned my attention to the list. Apart from all the items on the previous contract, I couldn't see much else to approve. I navigated to the clipart in the document and placed one giant tick over the entire thing, eliciting a chuckle from

Connor that vibrated through my body as he wrapped his arms around me and pulled me near.

***

The following day was the first under our new contract, and I had a to-do list pinned to the fridge. As soon as I woke up, I went to check it out. If there was one thing that made getting out of bed in the morning easier, it was that I didn't need to go to work. The pile of pancakes waiting for me in the oven weren't bad either. Connor made breakfast before leaving.

I munched on one chocolate chip pancake while reading through the list on the fridge. Connor hadn't helped me write it, but I'd shown it to him after I wrote it. He approved wholeheartedly, and that's when he stuck it on the fridge for me. Perhaps I would be more productive if I composed such lists on a daily basis. As it was, I had quite a few things to do.

Eating was first, and showering was next. After that, I had to clean the hutch and feed Cloud. I hurried through my breakfast and raced toward the bathroom. Yet another benefit of living with Connor was that his shower was big enough that I could sing to my heart's content. I only ever sang and danced when he was at work though. I wasn't quite confident enough to let him hear me.

It occurred to me after I'd showered and put on some adult clothes, a pair of jeans and a black tank top, that life truly had improved since Lisa's vindictive act. I never expected it, but I was living the life of my dreams. The only thing that kind of sucked was the job hunt. That was the biggest thing on my to-do list, as it had been every single other day. I didn't know how there were so many jobs posted on a daily basis, and yet, no one had called me back. A part of me began to wonder if people were calling my previous employers. It would explain an awful lot.

I didn't like that thought, so I shrugged it off and headed to the garden, where Cloud was happily sleeping in her hutch.

"Hey girl," I murmured as I pulled her out.

She curled up closer in my arms, not yet ready to be woken up.

I set her down in the grass so she could run around for a bit, something I was only allowed to do if I supervised her and got down to cleaning the hutch. The only problem was that Cloud did not want to run about. One would think a rabbit would be happy for the chance to bounce around, but no. She was quite content to watch me. She was the stillest rabbit I'd ever seen, and it was hard not to notice how different we were. I struggled to stay still for too long. That might have been why Connor gave me so much to do at home, especially since I didn't have a job.

"You're a strange girl," I shook my head, replacing her bed with a clean one. Next, I picked Cloud up and took her inside so that I could fill up her water and food bowls. Only there did she start hopping about, making her way over to Connor's sofa and sniffing at it before moving toward the CD rack. The first time I'd seen his collection of CDs, I asked Connor how old he was. He laughed, but I knew I'd offended him when he started explaining that most of them belonged to his mother. That explained the Neil Diamond.

When I was done putting the food and water back outside, Cloud decided she didn't want to go back in her cage. She hopped out of my way every time I went toward her, and for a rabbit that didn't spend much time inside, she seemed to know exactly how to get away from me. I chased her for several minutes until a stitch formed in my side, reminding me just how unfit I was.

"That's it," I gasped, making my way back into the kitchen. I knew I had Cloud the moment I entered the living room because her nose began twitching like crazy. I waved the carrot around in the air, dangling it quite literally.

"Do you want it?" I said.

Cloud's nose twitched, and she took one hesitant hop toward me and then another. Getting down on my haunches, I simply took tiny steps toward her until we met halfway. As cute and fluffy as she was, Cloud did not mess around when it came to carrots. She chomped it out of my hand forcefully and began devouring it.

With a grin on my face, I took the chance to pick her up, careful to catch the end of the carrot so that she didn't drop it.

"I think that's enough excitement for one day," I murmured as I put her back in the hutch. I sat with her for a while, gently stroking her soft fur and mentally thanking Connor. If not for Cloud, I knew I'd be a rather lonely Little while he was at work.

Chapter 11

The days passed by and with them, the seasons began to change. Fall had come, bringing with it overcast mornings that made me want to stay in bed and watch movies all day. The shades of amber could be found everywhere, including in the brand-new necklace Connor bought me.

"It suits you," he commented.

"I always thought you'd be more of a spring girl," he said. I raised my eyebrows.

"With the way, I don't want to get out of bed?" I questioned.

"Fair enough, you've got me there. Can I see what you're painting?" He asked. We were in the room where all my Little things were kept. It became a den of sorts, similar to Connor's study. This was where I painted and wrote during the day. I inclined my head, and Connor came around to stand on the other side of the easel. The painting was a depiction of the garden outside, with orange and red leaves blowing in the wind along the grass. The old oak was devoid of leaves, leaning creepily with its branches curling like fingers. Cloud could be seen near the roots that broke through the ground, happily nibbling on a carrot. I could almost hear the rustle of the leaves as I looked at the painting. It was one of my favorites to date.

"Oh, wow," Connor murmured. I'd been painting every day as per my rules, and I could definitely see an improvement There was something genuine about Connor complimenting my art that made everything seem more real. I could always tell he was being honest.

"You really think so?" I asked, just in case.

"Jessie, I think you need to start sending your art to places. Let me help you create a portfolio and start sending it out," he said.

"You mean like, to galleries and stuff?" I was doubtful.

"I do. You've been looking for work for a while, right? You've technically been doing work every single day," he said.

I bit down on my lower lip, looking back at the painting. Maybe it wouldn't be such a bad idea after all.

"Okay. Will you help me?" I finally said. Connor's smile warmed my heart.

"Of course, I will," he said. We were silent for some time as I packed away my art supplies. Connor's return from work usually meant the end of my creative pursuits and settling into the sofa to watch something together. We didn't really do much else these days.

"Jessie, I wanted to talk to you about something," Connor started once I was finished.

"Did I do something wrong?" I said as I turned to him, instantly guilty.

"Why would you think that?" Connor asked as he shook his head and waved it off. "Wait, don't worry. You aren't in trouble," he said.

"Then what's going on?" I asked. He walked over to me, running a nervous hand through his hair.

"I've noticed that you've been a bit different these past few weeks. Apart from painting, you don't really do much else. I mean, there's nothing wrong with that, but…" He sighed, struggling to find the words. I heaved a sigh. This wasn't a conversation I thought would ever actually come up, and now that it was here, I wasn't sure how to tell Connor what was really going on with me. I went over to my painting seat, as equally at a loss for words as Connor had been a few moments earlier. The truth was nothing was wrong. We lived a perfectly good life. I might even get to have my art in a gallery if this portfolio thing went well.

"Please don't shut me out again," Connor said when I hadn't answered for a while.

"I'm bored," I blurted out.

"Bored? Bored with me?" His brows knitted together. Standing, I went over to him and took his hands.

"Of course I'm not bored with you, Daddy," I said. The look of sadness and confusion on his face broke my heart a tiny bit.

"I'm bored with life right now. When we first got together, everything was new and exciting. I miss that feeling. Take today for instance. I knew we were gonna go out there and watch something while snuggling on the sofa and while that's nice and all, I really miss the thrill of not knowing what was coming next. You know?" I tried to explain. Connor stared at me, and his silence only prompted me to talk more.

"I mean, we haven't been to another play party in a while. And sure, we changed the contract up, but that was months ago. Every day is predictable," I said. The tension in the room sparked, and my heart got a bit faster with each second that ticked by in silence. I hoped I hadn't said anything wrong. I wanted to simply ask Connor to say something, but of course I couldn't do that. So, I sat in my seat, watching him and sweating from nervousness.

"Well, how are you feeling about us?" He finally asked.

"Oh, Daddy, there's nothing wrong with us. I still love you. I just want a little more excitement, you know?" I said. Instead of answering me, Connor walked over and cupped my face with his hands. He leaned in and pressed his lips to mine. The suddenness, the pure passion of his kiss, made butterflies swirl in my stomach. I reached for his waist and pulled him closer, giving into the kiss with a small sigh in the back of my throat.
When he pulled away, I was breathless, and my lips felt swollen.

"I love you too," he whispered. Before I could freak out, Connor leaned in and dragged his lips along my neck, making me forget how words worked.

"I love you, little one," he said again.

"Daddy," I murmured. I couldn't believe I told him I loved him. I smiled demurely, feeling as if I could have floated upward and off of my chair in that moment. My heart was happy. I was happy.

"So, what do you think you're looking for, little miss?" He asked.

"It's been a while since you called me that," I commented. He gave me a moment to think it over.

"I guess, you know, some stuff to spice up our relationship. I... Uhm, I read about, like, impact play," I said smirking.

"Impact play?" Connor said, raising an eyebrow.

"Yeah, and uhm... Also like, training. Stuff like deepthroating," I stammered. It was so much easier to think and read about it than to talk about it. With every word I said, my neck got hotter and hotter. I was glad my hair was loose for the simple fact that it covered my ears because I was pretty sure they were as red as tomatoes.

"You want me to train you?" Connor finally asked. I bit down on my lower lip, nodding.

"You know, I happen to have a paddle in my bedroom if you really want to play with impact," he said.

"A paddle?" I breathed. Connor nodded his head, staring down at my lip.

"Wait here. And take your clothes off. I'll be right back," he said. My heart was racing as he ran off. I paused only for a moment before taking my top off. The next thing to go were my jeans. I couldn't waste a second. I may have wanted to try impact play, but I wasn't sure how much pain I could handle. It was better not to disobey my Daddy.

When he came back into the room, Connor held a bright purple paddle in his hand.

"Good girl. Bend over the chair," Connor said.

"Yes, Daddy," I said gulping as I did as I was told. I took a deep breath, telling myself that this was all about trust. If I didn't trust him, there was no way this relationship would work. Connor didn't smack me suddenly. I felt the paddle brush against the curve of my ass, cold enough that I flinched away from it. Connor paused until I settled back again. Without warning, the paddle came down on my ass, warm and hard. It barely felt like anything. Connor repeated on the other side before coming back. He was true to his word. Each spank was soft and gentle, but the longer he went on, the more it stung.

I almost didn't notice that they were getting harder and harder, but I knew without seeing it that my ass was bright red. To my utter surprise, my pussy was so wet it was dripping down the inside of my thighs. Each time Connor brought the paddle down, I could feel the sensation hitting me right in my center, in my most sensitive of parts.

"Are you okay?" Connor paused, right when I thought I wouldn't be able to handle anymore, and my safe word was hanging off the tip of my tongue. I nodded.

"Sweetheart, I'm going to need you to use your big girl words," he said.

"Yes, Daddy!" I cried out, clenching my ass cheeks. Once Connor stopped, all feeling returned to me.

"Do you want to stop?" Connor asked. I

nodded my head, which awarded me with Connor's gentle hands as he stroked my ass comfortingly.

"Do you want to do something else?" He asked.

"I want to suck your cock," I whispered. I didn't usually speak dirty. That was Connor's job.

"Ask for Daddy's permission," he said. Something about the fact that I couldn't actually see him made me even hotter: my pussy pulsed and I moaned. I took a deep breath before I spoke.

"Daddy?" I asked.

"Yes, baby girl?" He sounded as breathless as I did.

"Please, can I swear?" I asked.

"Just this once," Connor whispered as if he were afraid of breaking the intensity of the moment. My pussy clenched again.

"Please, can you fuck my throat?" I asked.

"Oh, God, little one," Connor moaned. He moved around in front of me and unbuckled his belt and jeans, freeing his hard-on. It bounced out so excitedly that I giggled and that only drove Connor crazier. I could see it written all over his face as he reached forward to stroke my hair.

I looked up to find that he was checking out my ass, still on display in this bent-over position, while holding his cock in one hand. He moved forward until the head touched my lips and I opened my mouth eagerly, allowing him to slide in until he reached the back of my throat in one smooth movement.

It was impossible not to gag, and the second I did, Connor pulled back slightly. I swirled my tongue all around his shaft, paying special attention to the underside. All the while, I kept my eyes glued to his facial expressions. My favorite part about sucking Connor off was the pleasure that it gave him. Don't get me wrong, other things did that too, but there was some kind of power that came with having him in my mouth. It was the one part of the relationship where I felt truly in charge, the one part where I didn't choose to give him all the control.

"Oh, you like that, do you?" Connor whispered.

"You like Daddy fucking your throat? You're such a good little girl," he added. My pussy responded to his words, and I sucked even harder. Drool dripped down my chin, but I didn't care. I wanted him to know what his words were doing to me, what he was doing to me.

"I want you to relax, baby girl. When I move forward, just relax and breathe through your nose like you normally do," he said. I tried. As hard as it was, my body felt overloaded with sensation, I relaxed. I breathed through my nose. Connor took slow, shallow thrusts while I did, letting me get used to it.

"That's it," he commented in his proud-of-you voice, stroking my hair with one hand. The other reached forward and slapped my ass cheek. He muffled my cry as he reached over and repeated the action. His arms were so damn long that he could reach my pussy while in my mouth. I couldn't help lifting my ass up so he could get a better angle, which in turn made him slide into my throat.

Connor was fully in my throat; every last inch of him buried in my mouth. My eyes widened as his balls touched my chin, and he released a grunt of pure ecstasy. At the same moment, I felt two fingers slide into me easily. This was the wettest I'd ever been, and I could barely contain myself. Somehow, his fingers pumping in and out of me made me want to suck his dick even harder and so I did, eliciting yet another groan.

"Oh, fuck," he murmured. And the next thing I knew, Connor was pumping in and out of my mouth like a piston. I could do nothing but take it as he used my mouth. Sometimes I gagged, and when I did, he pulled out for only a moment to let me catch my breath before reentering. More often than not, he made it easily into my throat. I couldn't keep my eyes on him anymore; they were shut as he fingered me as fast and hard as he was fucking my mouth. With every stroke, I could feel my orgasm building and the fact that I was letting

Connor use me while I reached the peak only made it hotter.

Connor reached forward with his other hand, releasing my head so that he could stroke and squeeze my ass while he fucked my throat. The moans I made around him, sending vibrations through the length of his cock, drove him crazy. I could tell because that's when his thrusts grew more erratic. My whole body was alight with pleasure, and I wanted to scream when I finally felt my body give in. Tiny sparks of electricity flooded toward my pussy and my cry of pure pleasure was drowned out by the cock in my mouth.

The second I came, Connor moved his hands to hold the back of my head. He stared down at my face as he pumped in and out and I knew it was because having me in this position, so vulnerable and willing, was exactly what was getting him off in that moment. I fluttered my eyelashes and sucked my cheeks in as hard as I could, the hollows obvious as I flicked my tongue along his shaft.

Finally, he began whispering my name and threw his head back, shutting his eyes as he forced his way forward one last time. I felt his cock twitch in my mouth, and then one, two, three spurts of his cum went straight down my throat. I had no choice but to swallow as quickly as I could, eagerly trying to gulp down every last drop as he sighed and moaned above me. Some of it escaped, joining my spit in dripping out of the corners of my mouth and down my chin.

When he slid out of my throat, he immediately got down on his haunches, so his face was level with mine. He cupped it and began showering my face with kisses before pulling back to look at me. He was beaming with pride.

"Are you okay?" He asked.

"Never better," I smiled back. I shifted and realized the chair had been digging into me slightly. Connor answered by kissing me on the lips, and I gave into his tenderness, closing my eyes and enjoying the moment until he broke away.

"You are such a good girl," he said as I giggled with pride.

"How about we get you bathed, huh? And I'll put you into a clean diaper, and we can cuddle," Connor said.

"Yes, please," I whispered. Connor led me into the bathroom and ran me a bubble bath, helping me climb into the warm water. He reached for a washcloth and gently washed away our session, the cum, and the pain. There was nothing sexual about this bath. Daddy was simply taking care of me, gentle as ever as he moved the washcloth over every inch of me. When he was done, he washed and conditioned my hair, making it into shapes that had me in fits of giggles that splashed him with water. His eyes were filled with love when he looked down at me, and I knew that he meant what he had said earlier.

After I was squeaky clean, Connor fetched one of the soft towels and held it out for me. He wrapped me up like a caterpillar and dried me off while I squirmed.

"Daddy!" I exclaimed.

"Do you want me to moisturize you, baby girl?" He asked. I nodded my head vigorously. Especially after spanks, this was one of my favorite ways to be cared for. Connor unwrapped me and got the moisturizer, lathering his hands up and rubbing down every part of me. He paid special attention to my butt cheeks, which I could feel were red from the spanks.

"Wow, sweetheart. Are you okay?" He muttered.

"I'm fine, Daddy. I liked the impact play," I replied.

"I wanna get dressed by myself tonight," I said when he was done putting a heart sticker right on the front of the diaper.

"Oh, you do? When did you become such a big girl?" He asked. I smiled, earning myself a raspberry on my belly. Connor ruffled my hair and went out to the kitchen. After that, I pulled on the first onesie I ever got and grabbed Peanut Butter before heading out into the kitchen.

A cup of hot chocolate was already waiting for me, steamy and creamy with marshmallows floating on top. I held my arms out and Connor, who had gotten dressed in my absence, lifted me up onto the counter, holding me in an embrace for a moment longer than he really needed to. Afterward, he passed me my hot chocolate.

"Careful. Use both hands," he instructed. I watched Connor bustle around the kitchen, preparing pancakes for us, and my toes curled with wonder. He smiled and walked over to me, brushing strands of damp hair out of my face.

"You know, our anniversary is coming up. I was thinking of taking you on holiday, maybe somewhere with the Eiffel Tower. What do you say?" He asked.

"Daddy! I love Paris!" I exclaimed.

"You do?" Connor leaned in to kiss the top of my head.

"Well then, Paris it is. But first, I want to get your portfolio out there into the world. My little girl is too talented to be cooped up in here," he said.

"You really think my art is that good?" I asked sipping my drink.

"Sweetheart, I want to tell you something, but you have to promise not to be mad," he said hesitantly. Connor ran a hand through his hair.

"I may have already sent one or two photos of your art out to a gallery in France," he confessed.

"What did they say?!" I set my hot chocolate down, staring at him.

"They loved it. They want to see your portfolio," he whispered. I was so excited I wanted to bounce up and down. I settled for a little dance on the counter, which made Connor smile affectionately.

"Oh, my gosh. Please tell me you're not joking," I said.

"That's why I want to take you to France for our anniversary," he said. Tears welled up in my eyes as I stared up at him.

"Daddy, you are perfect," I said, looking up at him.

"No baby girl, you are perfect," Connor said, kissing me on my cheek.

Who is Tina Moore?

Tina Moore has enjoyed the lifestyle of a Mommy Domme for several years. She began exploring kink and BDSM in her youth and found her love of being a strict Mommy Domme in early 2000. Tina Moore is now an author of many MDLG, DDLG and ABDL themed novels.

Follow her on:

Author Page on Amazon

Instagram @tinamoore.kdp

If you enjoyed this book, it would be much appreciated if you leave **a review on Amazon**.